NOTHING BUT TROUBLE

JUSTIN M. ANDERSON

PUBLISHED BY

 SIGMA'S BOOKSHELF

MINNETONKA, MN 55305
WWW.SIGMASBOOKSHELF.COM

Chapter 1

What am I going to do?

<u>Monday</u>

Things haven't been going too well lately at the lab, and that's an understatement! We've already gone through seventeen test subjects and are no closer to finding a cure for cancer than we were when we started. This sure is a stupid project! Speaking of stupid, so are the lawyers I have to deal with on a daily basis because we've been plagued with lawsuits.

Along with the lawsuits, the news media is starting to attack Helix Remedies with quite possibly the harshest stories I've ever read. Since when is the media allowed to do that? They make it sound as if we're terrorists or something when there are real ones they should be worrying about. We don't hold hostages or put fear in people. All we want to do is test out our medicines.

I'll never give up on human research. I'm strongly opposed to testing on defenseless animals. They're incapable of making important decisions for themselves. If they could, they'd say, "No way, human."

You wouldn't subject a child or mentally incapable human to testing. So why would you test on an animal? Animals shouldn't be regarded as disposable. If these drugs are going to benefit humans, they should be tested on humans. It only makes sense.

Okay, politics aside, maybe this approach has caused problems over the years. Take our Mood Hair Gel, for example. It was supposed to turn people's hair different colors depending on their moods. It actually worked, but too well.

One test subject's hair turned bright red and actually caught on fire when he got angry. He sued us for personal damages. He won the lawsuit, and that of course opened the floodgate. Many similar cases followed, and we lost all of them.

Then, of course, the negative stories followed. They led to tons of complaint calls about other Helix Remedies products on the market.

Sure, what we do here is dangerous, and sometimes deadly; but what everyone's forgetting is that nobody has been forced into our drug trials. They're told about the risks up front and given counseling to make sure they aren't depressed or desperate for money. They even have the option to quit at any time.

It's ironic. Our human testing program is packed to the brim with safeguards. We follow the codes and regulations to a tee. Why are we the ones getting all the bad publicity?

Why won't they single us out for the good things we have done, like standing up for animal rights and inventing the first diet plan for both people and their pets? (Seriously, I still can't believe nobody's done that before.)

But no. They bring up all the bad stuff, like the recent price increases on our lifesaving products. We wouldn't have had to raise prices if it hadn't been for the crippling losses caused by all those lawsuits. It's the public's own fault.

As if all of THAT couldn't possibly be bad enough, about

two months ago someone I call the Shadow Man approached me with an offer. One I should have refused and laughed at, then sent him on his way about.

He offered to give the company $5 million if we developed a successful cure for all cancers, something that would also restore our tainted reputation. He gave us a measly ninety days to figure out what humanity has been trying to do for centuries.

I must have been blind with relief because not too many weeks afterward, I realized that we were doomed. We don't have the resources, time, or money to find a cure for cancer. Create the cure and I'd receive vast funds and support. Fail to create it, and I can only guess what would happen.

I still don't know much about the Shadow Man, and he clearly won't reveal anything about himself. I'm tired of secrets and I'm tired of pressure. I really want to know who this guy is. The Shadow Man could be from a foreign government for all I know. But then again, he just seems too strange. I must note that I am the only person in the building who has ever talked to him or even seen him. That guy, and this project are driving me crazy! Seventeen test subjects later and we're still nowhere with this cancer cure project.

Our first test subject chickened out at the last minute. It turns out he did not like needles. When he learned that the treatment involved three daily injections, he couldn't even deal with the thought. Later, we figured out the cure we had developed wouldn't have worked anyway.

The latest test subject we had was a man who didn't actually have cancer. He was just a homeless guy who wanted to have a place to stay for a week. That sure was a waste of resources.

I won't go into too many details about the fates of the other test subjects in the study, but let's just say things didn't go any better with them. Anyway, the Shadow Man is supposed to be coming back to the office sometime this week. I don't know what I'm going to tell him. We haven't made any progress.

Sometimes I wonder if saving my company is really worth all this trouble. I want to get out of this mess, but is finding a cure for cancer too high of a price? But then again, what would I do without Helix Remedies? It's my livelihood. We must continue the effort at all costs.

Chapter 2

Skeletal Discovery

<u>Tuesday</u>

Today started out like most days. I arrived at work a little early, and did my morning walk through the underground corridors to the cafeteria. The concrete hallway twisted and narrowed as I made my way through it. Roaring ductwork and buzzing fluorescent lamps hung from the low ceiling. The corridor was dimly lit since most of the lights were burned out.

The Helix Remedies complex is what you'd call a unique space. The facility used to be the city hospital, and it had an entire wing dedicated to the mentally ill. It closed down suddenly in the 1960s without any explanation, then reopened as a medical clinic rather than a hospital in the 1970s.

According to the records I've seen, when the clinic owner decided to expand, it didn't make sense to renovate the building, so a newer, more modern clinic was built on the other side of town. The building had been empty with a For Sale sign in the window for a couple of years before I bought it and turned into the new headquarters for Helix Remedies.

My father founded Helix Remedies in the 1950s. It was originally a pharmacy that got most of its business from referrals made by Juniper General Hospital staff. Pretty ironic that Helix is now in the very building that once housed Juniper General.

I think it's a pretty neat place too. There are numerous underground tunnels that were used for transport between the buildings back in the day. Today they are just junk-filled corridors. But that's going to change. Someday we'll finally finish cleaning everything up, and then we can occupy the entire building.

I continued walking down the hallway. I pushed aside a creaky metal fire door and passed the familiar bricked-in wall that I see every day. That brick wall has been bugging me for a very long time. Ever since I bought the place, in fact. Well, I'll soon know what's back there. The construction crew I hired to open the sealed off areas should be over here any day now. They're almost done cleaning out the tunnels on the other side of the complex.

They've found a few interesting things in those other tunnels, including old computers, a lifetime supply of lab equipment, and long-expired medicines. There are also shelves upon shelves filled with small bottles containing every chemical compound known to man... all expired of course.

When I reached the end of the corridor, I climbed up a flight of stairs and found myself in the main hallway. Unlike the tunnels, this part of the building is warmly lit. Wooden panels line the walls. There are clay tiles on the floor and cheap 12" x 12" ceiling tiles overhead. As usual, I felt like I was trapped in the 1970s as I walked down the corridor.

Dozens of my employees were walking in all directions. There were some scientists pushing a cart of samples towards the elevator. I continued down the hallway to the cafeteria.

When I walked into the cafeteria for breakfast, there was quite a commotion. Alarms were blaring. Men in lab coats were yelling and running around with fire extinguishers. There was smoke everywhere. The distinct smell of burnt bacon and pancakes was in the air.

"Oh great," I thought to myself. "Marty burned my breakfast again."

"I'm sorry, Wilbur!" said Marty, as he ran up to me, appearing out of the smoke. "I got distracted again. I forgot to turn off the stove after breakfast was ready! Please forgive me!"

"I'm just happy you didn't burn the whole place down," I muttered to myself.

Looking after Marty, who I discovered living in an old boarded up office right after I bought the place, has been my secondary job here ever since I decided to take him in. What was I thinking? Oh yeah, I felt sorry for the kid. He was barely twenty-years-old, had been kicked out of his parents' house, and had no idea what he was going to do to make a living.

Well, he can cross cafeteria worker off the list. Maybe it's time to see if he'd make a good janitor's assistant. I need to speak with Tom about that. I sighed at the thought that I'd be limited to just a banana for breakfast that morning. I whipped out my phone and dialed Laurie down in Human Resources.

"Laurie, did you hear what happened?" I asked.

"Sure did Wilbur," she replied with a chuckle. "I'm going to post a job for a new chef in the lobby. Want it to be in the newsletter?"

"Sure, why not," I sighed. "Contact the marketing team too."

After thanking Laurie, I hung up and checked my e-mail. There were no real e-mails. Just junk. Did you know that you can buy swampland in Florida for only a dollar per acre? Or that you can increase your IQ ten times with just a single pill? Hey, that's a great idea for a product. I wonder if it would really work. Why did I let the staff put my e-mail address on the company website? That was a big mistake. Now every spammer on Earth has it. I angrily put my phone away.

"Well," I sighed, "this day is off to a great start."

"Is this seat taken?" asked Dr. Wayne Wagner, the chief physician in the on-site clinic.

"No, you're welcome to pull up a chair," I groaned. "That is if you think you can afford to be seen with a MONSTER!"

"Oh Sir, you're too hard on yourself," Wayne replied. "I don't think of you as a monster. You just need help proving to the public you're working to better society. But this project you have us all on, this search for a cancer cure, is not the way."

Dr. Wagner is a brilliant medical researcher, but probably an even better physician. I still can't believe we were able to steal him away from the local university. I knew we'd need his help when the Shadow Man came along. Though things would be much easier if he'd stop challenging me at every step and just acknowledge the man's existence. Since I'm the only one who has ever seen him, a lot of people think he is a figment of my imagination, but the Shadow Man is as real as you and me. I get the feeling that Wayne is one of those people who doesn't believe me.

Oh well, at least he's nice about it, unlike the rest of the executive staff. There are rumors floating around that some of them are planning a takeover. Luckily, I already planned for that. If any attempt is made to overthrow me, those involved will be fired immediately. I'm quite proud of myself for making that a rule.

Wayne must have noticed I was ignoring him, so he spoke up.

"On another note," he continued, "the excavation team has made a discovery you'll want to know about."

"What?" I demanded. "Why wasn't I informed about this?"

"It just happened. I was sent here to inform you."

"Oh. Right."

Wayne went on to describe the discovery. The remains of a strange creature had been found lying on its side in one of the abandoned tunnels. It was mostly bones, but there was some tissue as well. Suddenly, opening up the brick wall I pass everyday didn't seem as appealing anymore.

"Great," I sighed. "A body? Looks like another lawsuit is coming our way."

Wayne shook his head and sighed, "Just follow me, Sir."

We headed towards the elevator. As we reached the lower level, I started shivering, but it wasn't cold at all. It was actually quite hot down there. I found myself thinking about how our bad reputation was about to get even worse. Finding a dead body would not be good for us. My heart pounded as the doors creaked open.

Wayne and I walked out into the large, round tunnel ahead. The brick walls were coated with dust and graffiti that said things so nasty I can't repeat them. The floor was dirty and covered in litter. There were puddles of water along the walls, and it stunk to high heaven in there. I should have brought my boots and the gas mask I found in one of the tunnels a while back.

The only lighting in the area was from the construction team's headlamps. Along with the construction workers were several scientists and Tom, our janitor.

"So," I asked, trying to poke my head into the crowd, "what's this discovery of yours?"

A scientist named Jerry stood up. "Well Sir," he said, "we have no idea what we've found to be honest."

As I walked up to the carcass, the scientists gathering around it like vultures stepped aside to make room for me. On the ground was a headless skeleton with a little bit of flesh remaining. A shiver went up my spine and I looked away in an instant.

"H-How?" I asked nervously. "How can you even look at that thing?"

"I worked in a crime lab," replied a young woman named Brenda, who was clearly more focused on writing down notes then having a conversation.

Despite my initial disgust, I soon found myself staring at the skeleton again. In addition to the bones and tissue, I saw the creature also had spines, clawed hands, menacing taloned feet, and a… tail?!

To add to the confusion, there was no sign of a skull anywhere. "Where's its head?" I asked. "Did somebody chop it off and carry it away?"

"Your guess is as good as mine Sir," replied Philip, another scientist. He was holding a chisel and hammer.

Why was it so disfigured? Maybe they were doing some experiments here. Perhaps they were studying the effects of radiation on humans and this was some sort of horribly unlucky test subject. Thank goodness nothing like THAT ever happened at Helix.

The more I studied the skeleton though, the less human it looked. What the heck was that thing? The bones looked like they'd serve the same purpose as a human skeleton, but they were all shaped slightly differently. Why?

"Bill," I said to Dr. Harrison, the company's chief of genetics, "take this thing to the genetics lab and sequence its DNA. I want to know what this is."

Dr. Harrison's eyes looked glazed over. His brown hair was uncombed, and his safety goggles hung down his face. He probably got here at least three hours early. If anyone's been spending more hours on our cancer research project than Wayne, it's got to be Bill.

"That's already in progress, Sir," Bill yawned in his nasally voice. "I have someone coming down here right now as a matter of fact."

I heard splashing and rattling wheels as another scientist pushed a metal cart over the uneven floor. "How long will the sequencing take?" I asked.

"Well," Dr. Harrison replied, "assuming that this... thing has a similar amount of genetic material as a human, it should take the sequencing farm two days to process a sample."

"Alright. It better not be any more than that," I demanded. "I want those results right away! Do you think they'll find more of these things?"

"You never know, Sir."

Chapter 3

Nothing But Trouble

<u>Wednesday</u>

Last night the scientists extracted the remains from the tunnel. They have begun sequencing the creature's DNA from a small sample taken from the remains.

To me DNA looks like a bunch of jumbled As Ts, Cs, and Gs, but the scientists are confident they'll have an explanation for this skeleton when they're done sequencing its genome. They will look for similar tags between living animals and the skeleton, and try to determine its closest relative.

At the same time, the biochemistry team is doing its own investigation and hasn't found anything strange about the skeleton. Nothing special. It has a normal composition. It isn't radioactive or anything wild like that.

If the scientists do find anything, it surely wouldn't help us find a cure for cancer. That creature may be interesting, but it's not going to get us anywhere. We should probably just donate the old fossil to a museum; but I doubt that would do anything for our reputation either.

Anyway, when I came into work this morning, I found

an OSHA inspector wandering the halls. I didn't think they were due to come for another month.

OSHA has been after me for years, trying to find enough evidence to shut the place down. Yes, maybe we could work on reducing our annual accident count into the single digits, but we've gotten better. And as far as the place being in a state of disrepair, I blame the previous owners.

I also had a surprise meeting with one of our investors today. His name is Ethan Alexander and he had been one of Helix's best supporters. Mr. Alexander had always been especially interested in our efforts regarding allergy relief.

I was sitting in my office and sipping my coffee when I heard an urgent knock on the door.

"What is it?" I groaned.

Mr. Alexander opened the door and walked inside, carrying his briefcase.

"Welcome!" I exclaimed a little sarcastically when he came up to my desk. "Pull up a chair! Take a seat!"

Ethan was not in his usual cheery mood. He wasn't happy to see me.

"Mr. Watson," he sighed, as he sat down, "I have some bad news."

"Bad news?" I asked with a frown. "I already have a lifetime supply of it. I don't need any more."

Ethan sighed again and continued, "We have been informed of several recent lawsuits against Helix Remedies. Apparently, some of your test subjects and their families are suing for wrongful death and injury caused by what they call your ridiculous attempts at finding a cure for cancer."

"Wrongful death and injury?" I asked. "All of our test subjects had terminal cancers."

"That may be true, but many of these people would have been better off if they had never met you."

"Well those test subjects aren't holding up their end of

the bargain, now are they?" I replied. "I should be the one suing them!"

I opened up a file cabinet, pulled out a stack of papers, and slammed them down on the desk.

"All seventeen test subjects signed their name on a form releasing us from blame," I continued. "They knew what they were doing. We even gave them counseling to be sure! And just what is your point in coming here anyway? You're not my lawyer."

"I'm here because I don't think you're putting our money to good use," Ethan replied. "Your research has left behind a lot of angry people who want justice. These are human lives you're dealing with and I don't think you're taking this seriously. Due to your of your lack of compassion and morals, I will no longer be supporting your research."

That was it. I couldn't take it any more.

"GET! OUT! NOW!" I roared.

I wanted to shove the man out of the chair at that moment, but I didn't have time to. Ethan was so shocked at my reaction that he got up, snatched his briefcase, and made a run for it.

I slammed the file cabinet closed, then got up and slammed the door to my office. A glass frame with a newspaper clipping fell to the ground and shattered. That had been hanging up there since the place opened.

"Wonderful," I sighed.

I picked up the piece of paper, shook off the glass bits, and stormed back to the desk to put it away. I reached for my coffee, but some noises outside interrupted me.

Could it be the Shadow Man?

"Hello?" I called, but got no response. I got up and opened the door. Janitor Tom was outside sweeping the tile floor. He had his earbuds in and apparently had not heard me. "Tom?!" I demanded.

"Yes?" he replied, as he took out his earbuds.

"Would you mind coming in here for a minute?"

Tom slowly walked in with his broom. "I take it the meeting with the investor didn't go well," he said, looking at the pile of glass and broken frame pieces on the floor.

"It went really well actually," I sneered, as Tom began to sweep up the mess.

"Sounds to me like you can't afford another disaster," muttered Tom. "You must order the scientists to destroy that awful creature they found. They need to burn it!"

"Excuse me?" I asked, surprised at the janitor's advice. "What makes you so certain that we should destroy it?"

"They're nothing but trouble."

"What do you mean?" I asked. Tom did not offer a response. He finished sweeping the floor, and left my office without another word.

That was very strange. What did he mean by 'nothing but trouble'? And why does the skeleton need to be burned? What could be wrong with it other than the obvious? It's strange, it's dead, and it's missing its head. Hard to tell Tom's intentions. He has always been very cryptic in my conversations with him.

Oh well, I thought. Time to get ready for the budget meeting, so I can break the wonderful news. I spent the next few hours pouring through spreadsheets, trying to figure out where the money was going and how to divert it where I wanted it to go instead.

I discovered that there was too much money going to customer service. We had doubled the budget when we got sued the first time. Obviously it hasn't done anything to help the company so a few people over there will be packing their bags. The scientists in the hair lab can look for new jobs. The products they were working on have been off the shelves for months.

Our resident physicist can go back to the university. We haven't needed him all year. These were just a few of the many changes I made today that freed up a lot of money. I typed up the memo about what I wanted done, and walked it down to human resources.

"Laurie," I said, "I need you to take care of a few things for me."

I handed her the note and her jaw dropped.

"Half of customer service?" she exclaimed. "Without them, this place would be falling apart."

"They haven't helped much," I replied. "We're still getting lawsuits from unhappy customers."

Laurie continued scanning the paper.

"I agree on laying off the physicist. But not the people in the hair lab. What if you plan on making more hair products?"

"It will only be temporary," I replied. "All focus is on the cancer cure right now."

"Is that it?" asked Laurie.

"Nope, there are five more pages."

Laurie turned to the next page.

"Sir, you've made some questionable decisions during your time here, but canceling this year's ice cream social? What would your father say? He loved those. He held them every year, and I arranged just about every one of them for him."

"Don't worry, there will be another one next year," I replied, almost laughing. "I'll leave you to look at the next five pages while I get today's budget meeting ready."

I navigated the large maze of cubicles filled with people very busily entering data into spreadsheets. When I got to the physicist's desk, I found him taking a nap. Yup, he's going to be fired very soon too.

I made my way back to my office to prepare for the meeting. Thinking back to this time last year, the future looked much brighter. Last year we were celebrating the record-breaking sales of our water jet comb and looking forward to the launch of our Mood Hair gel. The final stages of testing and FDA approval were almost done. Not even a week later, a test subject's hair turned red and burst into flames when he got angry. He was left with second degree burns all over his body and an angry family. Wonderful stuff!

Because of what's been going on around here since then, I predict today's meeting is not going to go so well. The future is not nearly as bright.

Just a few hours later, I found myself sitting at the head of the table in the board room, playing with my coffee mug. Janitor Tom walked into the room to collect the trash from the garbage can. I was going to ask him about what had he said earlier about the skeleton, but he quickly left. I moved on with the meeting.

"Folks," I began, "I've asked you all to come here to let you know that our situation is dire. All the lawsuits that have been filed against us are taking their toll. Because of attorney expenses and the judgments against us, I am going to need to make some major changes to save the company. That means some of you are going to lose your jobs today. It's nothing personal. It's just business."

I paused and looked around the room and saw a lot of worried faces. I sighed and continued on.

"First off, we will no longer be offering paid internships in our labs. All the current interns will be informed of this new policy today and offered the opportunity to stay if they want to work for free. If not, they'll have to leave," I said.

One of the scientists in the back of the room asked, "Can I slip my interns a few dollars to keep them around Sir?"

"If you want to. As long as it doesn't cost the company anything."

I paused to let this decision get absorbed by everyone around the table, then dropped some more bombs.

"I will also be cutting the customer service department in half, and you Sir," I said, pointing to the resident physicist, "your job is being cut. I simply can't afford to have someone who is just taking up space on the payroll. It's been an awfully long time since we've needed you."

Dr. Bryan, the physicist had an embarrassed look on his face when I said that. It was cruel, but true. We hired him back when we started research on prosthetic limbs. Because that project is dead and gone, his paycheck should be too. He really hasn't been a contributing team member in recent years.

I waited until everyone was paying attention again. "I'm also canceling this year's ice cream social," I said. Everybody gasped and started talking at once.

"Sir, you've got to be kidding," said Robert, my financial advisor. Everyone in the room nodded in agreement.

I continued to go through the rest of the changes with my staff. Most of them were minor compared to the first few.

"Why didn't you inform us of these changes?" asked Robert. "You should have consulted with us first."

"The thought did cross my mind," I replied. "But I was certain that nobody here would agree with me. I had to take matters into my own hands. By the way Robert, try to have that budget projection on my desk by tomorrow."

He nodded slowly, and took out his calculator.

"Dr. Harrison?" I asked. "Have you made any progress on that skeleton?"

"We're still waiting for the sequencing farm to finish," he replied.

I directed my next statement to all the scientists.

"Those of you who are working on the cancer cure project, there should be some more money heading your way. Let's try as hard as we can to do the impossible. I'd really like it if you people hurried along."

"How much time did this 'Shadow Man' of yours give you to create the cure, anyway?" asked Dr. Wagner.

"Hmm," I replied, "I believe we only have thirty days left. I'm supposed to meet with him tomorrow. I'll ask then."

Everybody stared at me for a while. Dr. Wagner and Dr. Harrison especially looked nervous.

"Well, you know the drill," I sighed. "Questions? Concerns? Just schedule an appointment with yours truly or slip a note in the suggestion box outside my office. I guess I'll see you people next time. Some of you, anyway."

Everyone looked at each other and took that as a signal to get up. They all filed out except for Dr. Wagner.

"Wilbur," he said, "we need to talk."

"No time," I replied. "Sorry, Wayne!"

The door to the conference room slammed and I slumped in my chair. It seems like these meetings get shorter every time.

Chapter 4

The Shadow Man

<u>Thursday</u>

The next day began with a visit from what I like to call the "Government Agency of the Day." This time, a group of FDA inspectors showed up to inspect our on-site pharmacy. They found that most of our over-the-counter medicines were not fully FDA-approved. The bad news is that our on-site pharmacy is being shut down, we're being heavily fined, and the rest of our pharmacies are probably next. The good news is that I've discovered where half our lawsuits were coming from.

Oh well, I thought, as I sat down at my desk. Once we find a cure for cancer, none of this is going to matter. The Shadow Man told me that creating a cure for cancer is going to save the company, after all.

Whenever the Shadow Man shows up at Helix Remedies, we have no real meeting place. He just seems to appear when I'm alone in a room. What's really strange is that he can somehow open locked doors without breaking the lock.

I used to be convinced that he worked for the government, but that was before I began to notice his strange behavior. I don't know how, but he seems to have... powers

20

of some sort. I've had the locks on my office door changed three times already, thinking he somehow got his hands on the keys. The last time around, I had a fingerprint sensor installed on the door as well. Only my fingerprint should have been able to open the door, but that didn't stand in the Shadow Man's way. He still got in somehow.

My thoughts wandered back to business. I had to lay off all of the workers in the pharmacy now that it was being shut down.

Just as I was about to pick up the phone to call Laurie, I heard footsteps coming from the shadows.

"Hello Wilbur," whispered a cold voice.

I looked up and there he was again, hovering right over my desk: The Shadow Man. He was dressed in his usual black business suit. He didn't have any hair. His face was pale, he had gray eyes and he was shockingly thin.

"Alright. What do you want this time?" I demanded, annoyed that my privacy had been violated again. "And how did you get in here?"

"How I got in here is only for me to know, Wilbur."

"Can I ask why you're here?"

"We thought you would have found the cure by now, so I have come to give you a hint."

"And what is that?" I said sarcastically. "The cure is right in front of me?"

"You could say that," the Shadow Man replied. "The cure exists. And it is not far from here."

"You mean it's been here all this time? You couldn't have possibly made it this easy."

"Finding the cure is but the first of many challenges you will face."

"What is that supposed to mean?"

The Shadow Man turned around and headed for the door. He opened it and looked back at me.

"You'll soon find out," he whispered. "Follow me."

I shook my head and got out of my chair. Here we go again. He knows his way around the place better than I do.

The Shadow Man led me out of my office, and into the quiet hallway outside where the receptionist had his feet up on his desk. That's very unprofessional behavior I thought. I'll have to remember to have him fired.

I followed the Shadow Man to the nearby elevator, which began moving on its own as soon as the doors closed. What was really strange was that none of the buttons lit up. The elevator descended away from the offices and down to the lab floor.

When the doors opened, I followed the Shadow Man into a busy hallway. There were people running everywhere. A few looked up at me, but as usual, nobody seemed to notice the Shadow Man. Either reality has been twisted, or I'm going nuts. Everyone except me thinks it's the latter.

We made our way down the hall, then turned into the lab where the skeleton of the creature was being kept. I now knew for sure the skeleton had something to do with this.

The room we entered was dimly lit. It was filed with cabinets and desks. Microscopes and other instruments were scattered about. A scientist was seated at each chair. All of them were hard at work.

Dr. Harrison and his team greeted me. They said nothing to the Shadow Man, again confirming that he was invisible to everyone else.

"Hello Sir," greeted Dr. Harrison. "Excuse me for saying this, but we're kind of busy at the moment."

I saw the skeleton lying on a metal table on the other side of the room. A scientist was holding a device that shined a bright blue light on the creature.

"Bill," I said to Dr. Harrison, "I have a question."

"I have an answer Sir," he replied. "Just make it quick."

"Is the genetic sequencing farm finished?"

"Yes, Sir," replied Dr. Harrison. "I was going to have those results on your desk by tomorrow."

"Well, I want them now!" I demanded.

"A long string of letters? I think it can wait."

"Was there anything unusual about the creature's DNA?"

Dr. Harrison scratched his chin as we walked over towards the skeleton. The scientist with the device grunted and left to return to his desk.

"Right… There was, as a matter of fact," Dr. Harrison replied. "My team hasn't been able to match it with anything in our database. Without a doubt, I can say that the creature we found in the tunnel was not… human."

"Well could this be some sort of ape?" I asked. "Maybe something left over from the Ice Age?"

"If this was an undiscovered primate species, we would have seen some comparable base pair sequences to primates, or maybe anything on this planet. We did not."

I sighed. He was starting to get into one of those explanations that went way over my head again.

"We also didn't find this in a rock. We found it on the floor," Harrison continued. "It's no fossil. Carbon-14 dating has revealed that this thing died about seventy years ago, give or take a decade."

"So you're saying this thing was alive when this place was a hospital?"

"Yes, Sir."

A feast of questions started going through my head. Where did Juniper General get something like this from? Why was it stuffed underground in the tunnel? And where is its head?

"I can't help but wonder what this thing looked like," I said.

"Well," said Dr. Harrison. "I could crank out the old facial reconstruction software if we-"

"Had the skull. I know. But why do you think it's missing?"

"The excavation team thinks that it might have been broken while they were excavating. I have some people down there trying to find it now. Anyway, I really need to get back to work, Sir. As interesting as your questions are, they're huge distractions."

"Alright, I'll let you get back to work."

I suddenly remembered the Shadow Man. I turned around, and saw him walking briskly towards the doorway. "Come back here!" I yelled. I tried to grab ahold of his jacket, but he had already stepped out of my reach.

"Sir?" asked Dr. Harrison. "Are you feeling okay?"

I ran past Dr. Harrison and shouted, "You're not getting away this time!"

I ran out of the lab, and the Shadow Man picked up his pace. He then rounded a corner. As I chased after him, all the scientists in the hallway stopped to stare.

When I looked around the corner of the hallway, the Shadow Man wasn't there. I would have been able to spot his black jacket in the sea of lab coats. All our meetings ended like this. He always walks away and vanishes when I stop paying attention to him.

I shook my head, and decided it would be best if I went back to my office. I got into the elevator, half expecting it to take me there on its own. This time though it worked just like a normal elevator.

When I arrived at the offices, I noticed that the receptionist not only still had his feet on the desk, he was sleeping too. I walked back into my office, and plopped onto the chair. I grabbed my phone to call Laurie down in Human Resources. That man needs some discipline.

I thought back to the Shadow Man before dialing Laurie. What does the skeleton have to do with finding the cure? And what are those other challenges he mentioned going to be?

Chapter 5

My Staff Thinks I'm Crazy

Friday

It was your typical Friday at the office. Lots of headaches threatening to steal your weekend away. I started the day with a cup of boiling water and all the coffee dust I could scrape from the machine. We had ran out of coffee beans.

Oh, and did I mention that our income has hit an all-time low? Wonderful. Full of wonder. I couldn't stop thinking about our miserably unbalanced budget, so I thought I'd give myself a break, and grab a bite to eat before getting back to work. I'm the CEO, right? I can take breaks can't I?

Later on, I found out that Marty is struggling with his new job as Janitor's Assistant. He made more of a mess than he cleaned up in the warehouse this morning. I think it's just a ploy to get back into the kitchen. I know for a fact that when he worked there, he was sneaking snacks throughout the day.

The pharmacy workers, and probably the receptionist that I fired earlier this week, are now protesting their firings outside the lab gates. They've gotten the attention of the news media. More bad stories about Helix are on the way.

I also can't get that skeleton out of my mind. I think that first thing Monday morning, I'll ask Dr. Harrison to start testing it. As vague as the Shadow Man was, I really think he was giving me a clue. What if the cure really does have something to do with the skeleton?

There is of course the risk that Bill will think I'm crazy. It's more than a risk, really. It's a certain danger. Everyone in this place thinks I've lost my marbles, but I don't care what they say. The Shadow Man is real.

Before lunch, I made my rounds through the hallways. Nobody understood why I was slowly peeking around each corner, quickly opening doors, and leaving without saying a thing. I was trying as hard as I could to figure out how the Shadow Man was able to get into the building without anyone seeing him.

Eventually, I ended up spotting him in the shadows at the end of a dimly-lit hallway. He was staring right at me. I couldn't see his face, but he must have been taunting me.

"WHAT DO YOU WANT!" I shouted. "Why don't you SHOW YOURSELF?!"

After I had finished screaming, he turned around and walked into a closet. I chased after him. I ran inside the closet only to find that it was filled with boxes of paper and a few computers. Suddenly, I heard footsteps coming from around the corner. I ran in the direction of the noises.

"HA!" I shouted. "I've got you now!"

A group of confused scientists looked at each other and stopped in their tracks. "You've got us?" asked Brenda. I swear she was rolling her eyes.

"What did we do, Sir?" asked Philip.

"Um...," I replied awkwardly. "Never mind, I thought you were somebody else. Sorry people. Get back to what you were doing." I headed to the cafeteria, and was very disappointed by the selection. Canned beans, water, and the kind of pretzel packets they hand out on airplanes. If that wasn't bad enough, today's special was protein powder made by the Helix Remedies nutrition lab. You can add it to your favorite drink.

I suppose that's what you get when you fire your chef. I'll have to start bringing home lunches from now on. That's what most of the staff does. I took my tray to my private dining room in back of the cafeteria and sat down. It was much more calming than the bustling cafeteria outside. The lights were dimmer too. Before I even had a chance to start eating, there was a knock at the door. It was Dr. Wagner.

"Wilbur?" he asked. "Can I come in?"

"Yes you may," I sighed.

Dr. Wagner wandered over to my table and sat across from me.

"So, Wayne," I started, "how's it going?"

"Not too well," he replied. "A few of my good friends lost their jobs when you shut down the pharmacy."

There was a long pause, which was interrupted by the obnoxious crunch of a pretzel.

"Wilbur?" he asked.

"What?" I murmured with my mouth full. "It's not my fault these pretzels are so awful."

"Wilbur?" he asked again.

"What's with the sudden first name basis? I'm still your boss."

"I refer to all my patients by their first names."

"I'm not your patient!" I snapped. "I'm your boss." I stood up and slammed my hands on the table. The dishes rattled.

"Today you're visiting the counselor!" commanded Wayne. "I have made an appointment for you for right after lunch."

"Oh yeah?" I said. "What's the urgency?"

"Sir, you have been acting very strange lately," said Wayne.

"I just received yet another report from some scientists who saw you running through the halls yelling after someone who wasn't there. You've also been firing dozens of people who didn't do anything wrong. It's time to do something about it."

"Oh, So that's what this is all about!" I snapped, raising my voice. "You're trying to overthrow me by making it look like I'm not fit for my job! Well, you know the rules! It's time for me to fire yo-"

"No, Wilbur! That's not it at all! There's no conspiracy!" replied Wayne. "I'm worried about you. The staff's worried about you. We're trying to help you and the company."

There was another awkward pause.

"So," I finally replied, "if I agree to this counseling session, what is in it for me?"

"What are we ever going to do with you Wilbur?" Wayne sighed, putting his face in his hands.

Realizing how strange my recent behavior must look to everyone else, I decided to make them happy and just go through with it. I didn't have anything scheduled that afternoon anyway.

After we finished eating, I got up and followed Wayne over to the medical wing of the building. I took a seat in the waiting room outside Counselor Jessica's office.

We used to have two counselors. That is until I fired them both and brought in Jessica, who seemed much more qualified than the previous two combined. She used to be a ship's counselor aboard the U.S.S. Enterprise, which is basically like a small town. I'm sure after her time on an aircraft carrier, she's heard everything.

"Wilbur Watson?" called a friendly voice. It was Counselor Jessica. She had just finished counseling a scientist, and was now standing outside her office.

"That's my name!" I replied.

"It's time for your appointment, Sir."

"Alright, I'm coming."

"Wayne, you can wait out here, or go back to your office, whichever you prefer," said Counselor Jessica.

"I'm staying here," said Wayne.

I stood up and followed Jessica from the waiting room to her office, which had a very homey feel. Inside the office was a fireplace, a desk, and two sofas. The brick walls were painted light blue. There was a picture of Jessica in a Navy uniform on the desk.

I sat down on one of the sofas. Before sitting down across from me, Jessica handed me a mug filled with mint tea, my favorite.

"Gee, thanks," was all I could think of to say. I was kind of nervous about what cognitive disease I probably had that Jessica was about to discover. There was a big stack of papers on her desk. I assumed she had been researching my "condition."

"Welcome, Wilbur," she started.

"What am I doing here and how long is this going to take?" I said abruptly.

"Well Sir, Dr. Wayne personally requested that I talk to you. It will be just a half hour. Why don't we start by discussing why you think he wanted you to see me."

"Well," I replied, "Wayne thinks I'm losing it and insisted that I come in for a counseling session, whatever that is."

"Wilbur," said Jessica, "a counseling session is used to determine what it is bothering a client. I am not here to diagnose you, but to help you."

"Great," I sighed. "Let's get this over with."

"Don't think of it like that Sir. This isn't a chore. It's just an opportunity for us to get to know each other better, and to figure out what's going on in your head."

"I got to know you well enough during your job interview

thank you very much. There's really no need to continue the conversation."

"That may be true, but now it's my turn to get to know you," replied Jessica, sweetly.

I grunted in response.

We talked about everything from my childhood to how I got started in business and the story behind how Helix Remedies came to be. As I told my story, Jessica nodded often and took lots of notes. I also noticed she was now holding the stack of papers that had been on her desk.

"Well," I told her, "my father owned a pharmacy called Helix Remedies. He would often bring me to work with him. Some days I'd count pills, and other days I'd make deliveries. When I would ask my father why some diseases can't be cured, he'd always reply: 'Every disease has a cure. It's just that nobody's found it yet.' Those words are the foundation of this company."

I then went on to tell her how our aggressive searches for "cures" had landed the company in trouble several times over the years. For example, there was a pain reliever that worked a little too well. Customers who took it often ended up with nerve damage. Some of them were even paralyzed.

I also talked about how much stress the search for a cure for cancer was causing. I told her why I had been firing so many people lately.

"I want to focus on this cure as much as possible," I said. "We need as much money as possible going towards it, so any reason to fire someone is a good reason."

I also told her all about the Shadow Man and how I've been seeing him everywhere lately. Jessica replied that I seemed to be obsessed with the cancer cure, completely forgetting the words I founded this place on: To Cure Every Disease.

"But that's still our mission," I argued. "We're just a little preoccupied with fixing our reputation."

"I'd say you're a little more than preoccupied," said Jessica. "You're obsessed."

"So what's my diagnosis?" I asked, with my hands on my cheeks.

Diagnosis?" she asked. "There's nothing wrong with you. You're just under lots of stress."

"That's what you want me to think, isn't it?! I bet one of those papers you're holding says that I'm insane! A paranoid schizophrenic!"

I snatched the stack of papers from under her notepad. To my surprise, they had pictures of different yoga poses.

"Me doing yoga?!" I yelled, tossing the papers everywhere. "Was that also Wayne's idea?!"

"No," replied Jessica. "I printed them for myself, but It may be a good idea for you too. Perhaps we could do yoga together."

"Me doing yoga! How ridiculous!"

Jessica eventually convinced me to try some weird yoga relaxation techniques. No idea how they are supposed to help me, but whatever.

When the session was over, she had somehow come to the conclusion that the Shadow Man was nothing more than an embodiment of all my hopes and fears. Pretty far fetched theory, as Dr. Harrison would say. Then again, Dr. Harrison would probably agree with the counselor. Everybody here thinks I've lost it.

Jessica announced that it was time to go home. "We've been at this the whole afternoon Wilbur, and I think it's time to call it a day. Let's meet here again on Monday. I need to get home to feed my kids."

Kids. Yuck. I don't like kids. Kids are creepy.

We said our goodbyes, and I headed back to my office. How "just a half hour" transformed into all afternoon, and then another counseling session next week is beyond me.

"How'd it go?" asked Wayne, as he looked up from reading the company newsletter. He had apparently stayed in the waiting room the whole afternoon.

"Very well!" I lied.

When I got to my office, I packed up my things and made my way home. I know Wayne and Jessica meant well, but I'm a busy man. I have a failing research company to run, and don't have the time for counseling sessions. I could have accomplished a lot this afternoon if I hadn't been stuck in a meeting with the company shrink, who is trying to convince me that the Shadow Man isn't real.

Jessica couldn't be more wrong. The Shadow Man is definitely real; and guess what else is real? The conspiracy to overthrow me.

Chapter 6

The Lab

Monday

That skeleton has been on my mind a lot lately. The Shadow Man gave me a clear hint that it has something to do with the cure, but what?

In order to find out, we need to start testing. I decided the time had come to cancel all the other projects we have in the works and start focusing on the creature. I suppose I don't need to fire anyone today. Those who don't have expertise in advanced biology should be capable of being lab assistants.

After breakfast, I decided to go the labs and ask Dr. Harrison and his team to start looking in the creature's remains for a cure. I left the cafeteria, and made my way to the elevator. It took five long minutes for the elevator to arrive. Its large gates slid open, letting out a few busy scientists, along with a man pushing a cart of nitrogen. I stepped inside, pushed the button for the first basement and headed to the main labs.

When I passed through the dust flaps at the entrance to the labs, nobody bothered to look up. Everyone was doing their own thing.

Some scientists were walking around. Others were doing lab work at their desks. They were busy looking into microscopes and delicately transferring specimens with eyedroppers. All the centrifuges in the genetics section were whirring and spinning samples

Air ducts and lamps hung from the ceiling. There were also pipes up there, which were labeled things like "Vacuum" and "Oxygen". Like most of the facility, the walls were made of red brick.

These labs stretch the entire length of the facility. Janitor Tom isn't too thrilled about the distance he has to travel to keep the place clean. Neither are the scientists who have to visit colleagues on opposite sides of the building. We'd buy some golf carts for them if we could, but right now that's not in the budget.

It took a few tries to get the attention of Dr. Harrison, who appeared to be doing three things at once, including ignoring his boss.

"Hello Sir," he said as he put down a calculator. "What brings you here? I'm awfully busy at the moment, so make this quick."

"Well, what you're doing now will have to wait," I said. My eyes trailed off as I spotted some scientists looking through microscopes and jotting down notes. "I have plans for the skeleton."

"Plans for it?" asked Dr. Harrison. "Do you want to display it in the lobby?"

"No," I replied. "I want you and your team to look for the cure for cancer within it."

"What am I?! A witch doctor?! We've always looked to plants and microbes for our medicinal needs. Using any animal is uncommon, and this thing we found is definitely out of the question! Without proper identification, we can't do anything with these remains."

"Isn't there still some tissue left you can test?" I asked.

"There is Sir, but we can't make miracles happen out of thin air," explained Dr. Harrison. "I'd rather not do this."

"It's the only thing we haven't tried yet," I replied. "What do we have to lose?"

"Alright Sir," Dr. Harrison sighed with annoyance, "we'll get started, but keep in mind nothing like this has ever been done before. I don't quite know where to start. Don't get your hopes up too high."

"I'm afraid I have to," I said. "We are running out of time!"

"Running out of time for what?!" asked Dr. Harrison.

"The Shadow Man gave me a time limit of ninety days to find a cure, and we only have thirty left."

"You said thirty last week!"

"You're right. Make that twenty-five days left to find the cure and deliver it to the Shadow Man."

"The Shadow Man..." Dr. Harrison muttered, shaking his head. "Now get out of here! Because of you I am now extremely busy!"

I never did much with science past high school, but it's clear that Bill was right. We are attempting the impossible. The chances are slim.

I've asked Bill's genetics team and the rest of the lab techs to work around the clock. They aren't too thrilled about it.

As for myself, I'll be staying late with them to monitor their progress. I'll be extra sleepy when morning comes, but at least I can still have my morning coffee. We may be almost out of money, but we still have several tin cans filled with coffee dust left thank goodness.

A lot of my employees keep coming to my office with their heads full of questions. I don't think I should have ever announced to the staff that the Shadow Man had offered me a deal.

They are so skeptical that even two months later, they are still asking for proof of the Shadow Man's existence. That must be why Wayne signed me up for counseling sessions. Counselor Jessica is nice and all, but give me a break! She thinks I'm hallucinating! It's as if I told everyone that I had seen a ghost. I guess that man might as well be one.

If we find a way to finish our end of the deal. I'm willing to deal with a little more confusion, I guess. But Dr. Harrison is right. We can't make a miracle happen out of thin air. We need one.

Chapter 7

First Amendment Rights

When I drove to work this morning I was greeted by a traffic jam, so I decided to take the back way to the office. When I arrived, there were dozens of protesters picketing outside the main entrance.

Oh great, I thought. They've finally caught up to me. After all these months of threatening to make a big stink, it's finally happening. My former employees were upset over being fired. Some of our angry customers were there too. So were some of the test subjects and their families. They were protesting against human experimentation, which we've been doing here since day one.

I can't stress enough that I am an animal lover and don't think it's right to do experiments on creatures that are unable to decide for themselves if they want to participate. I have two cats and an iguana at home. Three of the most calm, loving pets you'll ever meet. I would never test on them.

After I parked my car in one of the warehouses, I made my way towards the main entrance. Even though I was wearing sunglasses, they knew it was me. There was no avoiding it. I had to face both the crowds and the media.

"Wilbur Watson," shouted one of the reporters.

"Over here Mr. Watson," shouted another.

I ignored them both. All of them in fact. I pushed my way through the crowd of protesters and reporters, all yelling at the top of their lungs. My heart pounded and the whole world seemed to slow down around me.

"Killer," shouted one of the protesters.

"Murderer," screamed another.

They also said a variety of other things I will not be mentioning here. I wanted to respond, but knowing whatever I said or did would end up on the nightly news, I decided to just push through the crowd silently until I safely made it to the entrance.

As I entered the lobby, the entire security team was huddled near the door, along with a few police officers.

"Aren't you going to escort those people off my property?" I asked, breathing heavily. "They're trespassing."

"Perhaps, but they do have the right to gather and protest," explained Officer Brian, my Chief of Security. "The First Amendment to the Constitution says so."

Right as he said that, the door pushed open and Dr. Wagner pushed his way inside.

"Well Wayne," I sighed instead of a simple hello, "I guess a lot of people are going to be late for work today."

"At least the protesters are being peaceful," said Wayne, as he adjusted his glasses. "They're just exercising and respecting their First Amendment rights to gather and protest."

"Peaceful?" I replied. "If you call disrupting my business peaceful, then perhaps you want to join them! And you say they're exercising their First Amendment rights? What about MY rights? These people are blocking the entrance and spreading lies! Arrest them, officers!"

A cop with a big mustache turned to me. "If any of them try to enter the facility," he said, "that is exactly what we will do. Until then, we'll keep a close eye on them."

"I think we need to hold an emergency meeting on this matter!" I demanded.

"That really isn't necessary Sir," said Wayne. "There's not much to discuss, and I'm guessing only half the staff will make it into work today. Just leave this in the hands of the officers."

"Fine," I replied. "You win."

I headed down the hall to my office. When I got there, Janitor Tom and Marty were mopping the tile floor just outside. "You missed a spot over there son," said Tom, pointing.

When Marty saw me, he dropped his mop and bucket, spilling soapy water all over the floor. "Oh, hey Wilbur!" he exclaimed.

He's not really doing to well as Janitor's Assistant so far. Here we go again, and since when has he been calling me Wilbur at the office? I told him to call me Sir.

Suddenly, Janitor Tom looked up at me and muttered something.

"What was that?" I asked.

"You must destroy that horrible creature," he said.

"Again, why?"

"I said it before, and I'm saying it again. They are nothing but trouble. They kill, they maim, and they have no regard for human life."

"Were those creatures alive when the previous owners were here?" I asked. "Were there more of them?"

"We did what we had to do to get rid of them and you should do the same before history repeats itself!"

"What happened?" I asked.

"That's all I can say," replied Tom, as he slowly walked away and began talking to Marty.

"Where do we need to go next, Mr. Janitor?" asked Marty.

"The main lab," Tom responded. "A scientist tipped over an entire cart of lab equipment. There's glass everywhere."

I guess I'll be firing that scientist, I thought to myself.

As Marty and Tom made their way downstairs, I went back to the lobby to check on the protesters. When I got there, it looked as if the crowd outside had doubled.

I also noticed something that seemed off. The guards weren't by the door anymore. They had all moved out to the parking lot. Should somebody have stayed behind? This isn't going to be good, I thought. The crowd had grown so large it seemed like it could pour inside at any moment.

I tried to push that image from my thoughts and returned to my office. I had a lot to catch up on. That counseling session took at least five hours out of my life. Okay, maybe three. Well actually, two. Regardless of how long it took, I don't feel any better. Jessica is a nice lady, but all I got out of the session is that she thinks I'm crazy.

When I got to my office, I decided to look at a progress report from the labs. I was not surprised to learn that Dr. Harrison hadn't even started testing the skeleton for a cure. My first thought was to fire him for ignoring my request, but I quickly realized that was a bad idea. Dr. Harrison, with his Harvard degree and tons of experience in genetics and cellular biology, was just who I needed on my team to help save the company. I decided to give him more time.

After reading the lab report, I turned my attention to the busy work waiting on my desk. I had to balance the budget and go through spreadsheets. The only times I left my office were for lunch and for restroom breaks.

Before I knew it, the day was over and it was time to go home. I packed up my things and left my office.

As I made my way through the hallway, I heard a big commotion coming from the lobby. Then I heard shattering glass, followed by screams.

"Get down!" somebody yelled.

When I peeked around the corner, I saw that the crowd was starting to pour into the lobby. It was exactly what I had feared would happen earlier in the day. Some of the protesters were carrying metal pipes and smashing everything in the room. One of them destroyed a lamp. Another smashed a computer monitor.

"How bad is it?" asked Dr. Wagner as he came down the hallway.

"See for yourself," I replied.

Wayne looked around the corner too. He immediately turned around and went the other way. I somehow felt the urge to stay and watch.

I thought I was hidden well enough until one of the protesters shouted, "There he is! Get him!"

"Oh great," I whispered, as the crowd began rushing towards me.

"Murderer!" shouted a man.

"He's a baby killer!" shouted an angry woman.

I snapped at that moment.

"You're full of lies! All of you!" I yelled, dodging a wide variety of objects. "I never wanted to kill anybody! I only wanted to help them, and in turn, help humanity! Is that too complicated for your tiny minds to comprehend?"

"You're the one full of lies!" shouted a woman. "I put my son's life in your hands and for what? Just another disappointment. You're a monster!"

"You just don't get it do you? Because of your son's contribution to science, we now know how NOT to cure cancer!"

The crowd closed in on me like a pack of wolves. They hissed and growled.

"Perhaps I should have worded that differently?" I asked, smiling nervously.

Realizing I was not going to win that battle I ran, fleeing into the janitor's closet. I slammed the door behind me, and immediately heard pounding on the door, or maybe that was my heartbeat. I thought I was dead for sure, but then a voice said, "Wilbur, over here."

I followed the voice to the back of the closet. I looked through a crack in the metal fire door. Marty was standing on the other side. Janitor Tom was there too, sweeping away.

"You'd think they would have kept this area in better condition," he muttered.

"Quick, Wilbur!" yelled Marty. "Come inside!"

I slipped through the crack in the door and locked it behind me. I found myself in a secret storage room right behind the Janitor's Closet. Marty sat down next to me, lit a lantern, and pulled out a deck of cards. "Hey Wilbur," he said, "up for a game of cards?"

"No thank you!" I replied. "I almost lost my company once in a game of poker!"

"I just wanted to play Go Fish," said Marty, innocently.

I nodded and Marty began dealing cards.

It wasn't long before I started hearing the voices of the crowd again.

"Monster!"

"Killer!"

"Baby eater!"

Wait. Baby... eater?

"Well, this place certainly isn't sound proof!" I snapped.

"No it's not," replied Tom, "I can hear everything they're saying and my hearing ain't even that good!"

Marty and I must have played cards for hours. I soon began to yawn, but I didn't want to fall asleep before making the day's journal entry.

"Does anyone have paper?" I asked.

Tom handed me a old Juniper General Hospital notepad. "Here you go, Sir," he said.

After I finished writing about the day's happenings, Janitor Tom made some garbage bags into makeshift pillows and sleeping bags. I slept on the cold concrete floor that night, as far away from the door as I could possibly get.

Chapter 8

What Lobby?

The next day I woke up to the jingle they play when the morning news gets started.

"Can you believe this?" asked Marty. "I found a working TV back here."

"Be quiet, would you?" I snapped. "I want to hear their lead story. It's going to be about Helix!"

"How do you know?" asked Marty.

I told him to look at the screen. Our logo was fading in as a graphic over the anchor's shoulder.

"Good morning and welcome back to Wake Up Juniper on NBT News! We begin today with continuing coverage of the Helix riots south of here. Last night we showed you police officers in riot gear firing tear gas at protesters who had broken into the building," said the female anchor.

"Eyewitnesses tell us that was the turning point in this conflict. The protest had been mostly peaceful in the parking lot until a small group of angry protesters threw rocks through the front window, then pushed their way into the lobby," said the male anchor.

"I don't think name calling is that peaceful," I commented.

"The protesters are angry at Helix Remedies because they claim the company's CEO, Wilbur Watson, has no concern for human life or rights. Records show at least fifteen of their test subjects have either died or been gravely injured after undergoing medical testing at their lab, which only does testing on humans," he continued.

Then the woman took over. "Between last night and this morning, we're told at least twenty people, who had managed to get inside the lobby, were arrested and taken to jail. The remaining protesters were asked to leave the property."

After hearing the news report, I assumed it was safe to leave our hiding place and return to the lobby. Janitor Tom and Marty followed me. I opened the metal fire door, and walked into the janitor's closet.

I was afraid of what I would find behind the splintered closet door. My hand trembled as I reached for the rusty handle. The door was difficult to push open. It felt like it was being blocked by something. I knew this wasn't going to be good.

Once I had the door opened enough to climb out, I was greeted by quite a mess. The lobby no longer remotely resembled a lobby. Somebody had torched the receptionist desk. The light-up Helix Remedies logo was hanging off the wall, sparking. The drop ceiling was destroyed in places. Insulation was hanging down and there were ceiling tiles all over the floor. Janitor Tom immediately grabbed his broom and began sweeping up the mess.

"Well, this place 'ain't gonna fix itself," he muttered.

"This is what insurance is for, right Wilbur?" asked Marty.

"Can you believe this!?" I snapped, ignoring his statement of the obvious.

All the glass windows and doors at the entrance were shattered. A group of police officers was chatting by the entrance. When I emerged from the rubble, they stopped talking and looked at me in shock.

"Aren't you Wilbur Watson?" asked one of the officers. I recognized him as the County Sheriff. He had gray hair, glasses, and a large hat that shaded his face.

"Yeah, that's me."

"We thought you had been beaten by the mob and left for dead in the rubble. It's good to see that you're okay," said the Sheriff.

I couldn't read him. He seemed slightly disgusted, as if he didn't want me alive. I shook it off as he continued, "We would like a report of everything you remember to help us with the investigation."

"I'll have that ready later, Sheriff. Where are my employees?"

"A lot of people were trapped here overnight. They are being interviewed right now. One of them is a Dr. Wayne Wagner, who I understand saved several people from the mob last night," said the Sheriff.

"Good for him!" I snapped. "I bet he'll win a medal."

"Excuse me," said the Sheriff. "I need to speak with my deputies."

I kicked a piece of a coffee mug across the room. Suddenly, I felt a hand on my back.

"Hello, Wilbur," said Wayne. There was a long pause.

"Isn't this just wonderful!?" I asked.

"What?" Wayne replied.

"Are you blind? The lobby."

"I have to admit, those protesters did get a little carried away."

I started laughing hysterically.

"Carried away?" I asked. "You call this carried away? I'll show you carried away."

I picked up a piece of broken ceiling tile and hurled it at Wayne. "Ow!" he shouted, pushed back from the impact. "What was that for?!"

"I had to wake you up to reality! This is the absolute worst thing that has ever happened to me and you're just calmly shaking it off! Those rotten protesters have destroyed my life!"

Suddenly I heard laughing. It was the cops. They were mocking me. What did I ever do to them? Why is everyone against me? I stormed off towards the group of chuckling police officers, laughing like a pack of hyenas.

"And what are you fools laughing about?!" I asked. "This is not a laughing matter! This is going to cost me thousands of dollars just to clean up!"

"Calm down, Mr. Watson," replied the Sheriff. "We are not laughing at you. We are laughing about something George just told us about his baby boy."

I turned my attention back to Wayne and marched back over to him. "Stop acting so calm! We need to do something about this!"

"Do what?" asked Wayne. "What do you expect us to do? This place is a mess. It's clear we can't exactly sweep the debris under the rug and start up the human testing again right away."

"And that makes you happy doesn't it?!" I snapped. "Heck, maybe it's your ultimate goal to see my company fail and watch me suffer! All of you have been against me from day one, just waiting for me to fail so you could swoop in and take over my company! You're nothing but traitors!"

"Wilbur, enough of this nonsense! Nobody on your staff wants to see you fail! Nobody wants to take over Helix!"

"Everybody hates me, Wayne!" I replied. "Why would my staff be any different?!"

"Wilbur. They don't hate you. In fact, a lot of people feel sorry for you. They wish you could understand the harm in what you're doing."

There were a few moments of silence. Then Wayne continued on. "Can you remember the last time you visited with a test subject's family? I can't think of one. The reason the protesters don't like you is because you're not showing compassion. It's why our biggest investor walked away on us. Change your attitude and maybe people would start trusting you."

Then he said something that seemed to come out of nowhere. "Maybe human testing isn't the way to go," Wayne exclaimed. "And while you're at it, stop firing people at random! Making space on the payroll is not going to speed up the cure!"

"I fire people because they're not being good employees, just like how I'm going to fire you if you keep criticizing how I run this company!"

"Wilbur, human testing at Helix isn't going to ever have good results. You're not willing to put in the effort to make it work. It's just too risky, and your Shadow Man's advice is no reason to risk lives. He's not even real."

The Shadow Man? Not real? At that point, I lost it. I'm shocked I even remember my next words.

"You're lying!" I yelled. "The Shadow Man is as real as anyone in this building. You think I'm crazy. I bet you'd just LOVE to see me behind bars, wouldn't you?!" I screamed even louder. "IT'S NO SECRET YOU THINK I'M CRAZY! EVERYONE ON THIS PLANET THINKS I'M CRAZY!"

There was complete silence. Dr. Wagner obviously had nothing to say. He didn't even shake his head or sigh. He just stared at me for the longest time, and headed towards the elevator.

"Wayne?" I croaked. I could hardly get a word out. He looked at me one more time before walking through the broken doorway.

Chapter 9

The Train

<u>Thursday</u>

It seems like things are going from bad to worse around here. The protesters may be gone, and the police investigation is wrapping up, but that doesn't change what happened to my lobby.

The contractors had to stop excavating the tunnels, so they could put all their effort into fixing the lobby. All of the windows are broken, so we're using plywood until I can fit new windows into the budget. The facility is now closed to the public. I've posted two armed security guards at the gates, so only employees can get in and out.

I was sitting at my desk trying to read over the incident reports. The losses are astronomical. Not only do we have to replace the windows, but we need new computers, new carpet, a new receptionist's desk, and a new custom sign. We're talking at least $50,000 in damages.

I forgot to mention that the ceiling was full of asbestos, which violates the building code. I'm getting fined for that too. Even if my insurance company does cover our losses, the rates are going to skyrocket and it's not my fault. Those darn protesters have caused nothing but trouble for me. And

49

on top of everything else, now I also have to worry about the possibility of losing one of my best scientists.

Presumably because of me, Dr. Wagner has taken a few days off. He thinks human testing is a bad thing, but he couldn't be more wrong. I swear I'm going to prove the validity of this approach, and that the Shadow Man is real, even if it kills me.

I looked down at my watch and saw that it was nearly ten o'clock. Marty would be running up to me any second yelling the words, "Train! Train! The guys in the warehouse told me that a train is coming!"

Sure enough, that's exactly what he said not even five minutes later. "Wilbur!" exclaimed Marty, as he ran towards me. "Train! Train! The guys in the warehouse told me that a train is coming!"

"Alright," I groaned, "let's go."

Marty is pretty fixated on trains. He talks about them day and night and goes absolutely crazy when he sees them. You'd think he would have seen enough of them by now, as he has lived in this facility by the tracks for over a year. But no. He gets just as excited every time one shows up.

The train platform is one of Marty's favorite places in the world, and it's where all of our deliveries come in. We made our way over to the platform which is outside the Helix warehouse. It was a sunny day, but I wasn't in a sunny mood.

From the platform I could see the shed where my private passenger car is stored. It has been a long time since I've had it hooked up to a train. Once this is all over, I'll tour the country again, announcing that a cure for cancer has been found. I will be the most famous person in the world.

A smile was starting to form on my face when we heard the first horn. I actually started chuckling when Marty began to jump up and down like a little kid. Hard to believe he's in his twenties.

Soon the MESA locomotive pulled up to the platform and screeched to a halt. We've been a MESA customer ever since our new facility opened its doors. The engine's nose was orange and the MESA logo on the front was yellow. The rest of the engine was painted silver. The second engine was all silver and didn't have a cab.

"Oh wow!" said Marty. "That's an EMD F7. It's a 1,500 horsepower diesel locomotive that was built by General Motors in the early 1950s. I wonder why it's here. These aren't typically used as switcher engines. I have to go ask the conductor!"

"Not right now, Marty," I replied. "He has a job to do." The conductor climbed down from the locomotive. He was wearing an orange and silver vest, and was holding a clipboard. He walked onto the platform and started talking to the warehouse supervisor. Meanwhile, the warehouse crew worked to unload the boxcars. There were crates filled with lab glassware, chemical bottles and copy paper.

When I wasn't looking, Marty made his way over towards the men and entered the conversation. By the time I noticed, it was too late. The three men were engaged in a heated conversation about trains. I ignored them until I overheard them talking about the lobby.

"May I ask why the lobby is boarded up?" asked the conductor. "I saw it when we were rolling in."

Marty and the warehouse supervisor didn't get a chance to answer.

"It's being remodeled!" I snapped.

After the train left, I stormed back to my office to finish my work. I called Laurie in human resources.

"Morning," I groaned, angrily.

"I know, Sir," she replied. "You need me to deal with paperwork for another firing.

"Surprisingly, that's not why I'm calling," I replied. "I need you to send out a memo telling the scientists that they need to work weekends. We're running out of time to find the cure, and earn our $5 million."

"They're not going to like this very much," warned Laurie.

"I'm not in the business of making people happy," I exclaimed. "We have a world-changing cure to develop. Hopefully working overtime will allow us to find it quickly and trim a few days off our deadline. The Shadow Man is waiting."

"Okay Sir," Laurie replied. "I'll get to work on a new schedule. By the way Sir, I see that Wayne scheduled a counseling session for you. You're expected down there in the next twenty minutes.

"Forget that!" I snapped. "I don't have time for a counseling session today! Consider it canceled!"

"Sir, what are you going to be doing instead?"

"I will be observing the lab, making sure those imbeciles are doing what they're supposed to be doing!"

I slammed the phone down, and made my way to the main labs. When I got to the observation window above the lab, I saw Dr. Harrison and several men in lab coats. They were wheeling the headless skeleton into the room. Some of the scientists were at their workstations and others were carting equipment around.

"Okay people," sighed Dr. Harrison. "What tests haven't we done yet?"

"We could try sampling some bone marrow Sir," replied one of the scientists, scratching his beard.

A big smile formed on my face. The staff was showing signs of interest in the project. Despite the horrible last two days, everything was finally going according to my plan.

Chapter 10

The Cure

<u>Friday – One Week Later</u>

I haven't written in a while. I've been busy making sure the scientists stay on task. We didn't accomplish much last week, so there was nothing to write about. For the past few days I've been working very late hours and sleeping on the couch in my office. My quiet office was disturbed this evening when there was a loud knock at the door.

"Who is it?" I asked.

There was no answer. Could it be the Shadow Man? No. He never knocks.

"Can this wait?" I asked. "Someone in this room might have a budget to finalize."

The knocking continued. I wondered who could possibly be bothering me this late at night.

"Fine," I sighed, "I'll be right with you." I opened the door, and Dr. Harrison entered my dimly-lit office. He looked very nervous.

"Can I have a word with you, Sir?" he asked.

"Sit down, Bill. What gives you the wonderful idea of disturbing me this late?"

Dr. Harrison sat down, and handed me a clipboard.

"Sir," he said. "My team has found something in the remains that could help create a cure for cancer. "

My mind filled with excitement. Did he really do it?

"What is it?" I demanded. "Tell me your plan!"

"You see," he started, "while we were looking at a cancerous lung tissue sample from the creature under a microscope, we spotted something strange. Not only did the creature have cancer, it was fighting back."

"What? How?"

"We found what looked like a battle frozen in time in the sample we looked at. Kind of like my father's Civil War display in his basement. We were able to determine that unlike human white blood cells, the creature's cells were built to target cancer. Almost like an amoeba or separate organism, they could travel virtually anywhere in the body. They did this through the use of special microtubules that expanded and contracted allowing them to travel through tissue. What's most significant about these cells is that they could produce an enzyme that allowed them to eat through and neutralize even the toughest tumors."

"Now how do we turn that into a cure?" I asked.

"I was getting to that," Dr. Harrison replied. "Human white blood cells can't naturally target cancer. Though there have already been successful attempts to cure blood cancers, such as leukemia, by using genetically modified T cells to target the cancer."

That didn't sound right to me. "What?" I asked with confusion. "You said that the creature's cells could target any cancer and the Shadow Man insisted that our cure targets ALL cancers! I even wrote down a transcript of what he said!"

"Need I remind you that I'm talking about a cure that already exists? Now if we modified this natural cure we found, we'd start by extracting some T cells from a patient, put in the creature's genes, program them to target a tumor, and put them back into the bloodstream."

"You are a genius! Have you tested it out yet?"

"Yes, as a matter of fact. I recently experimented with a few live T cells I had lying around. They came from our previous test subject. I simulated some blood in a petri dish. As of today, those modified white blood cells have made their way into a clump of cancer cells. We believe the tumor is beginning to break down."

"Like an army storming a fortress," I replied.

"An appropriate analogy, Sir."

I grabbed Dr. Harrison's shoulders and shook his body.

"Has this been done before?" I asked excitedly. "I'll bet we're the first! Do you know what this means, Bill?"

I almost wanted to break into song.

"But, Sir-"

"We are going to get our fame and fortune back! We'll be in the history books! We're gonna get filthy rich! I can't believe we've finally found it! You gotta begin immediately!"

"Sir," said Dr. Harrison. "There's a problem with this cure."

My excitement died down along with my smile.

"Oh..." I sighed impatiently. "What sort of problem? You said it would work!"

"Hypothetically. We would be attempting something that's never been done before," he replied, "and we have no idea where the skeleton came from."

"Viruses are pretty scary too, yet we use them in vaccines everyday."

"That's different. We know a great deal about viruses. We have only begun to scratch the surface of this skeleton. There are far too many variables! Too many things could go wrong."

"Like what? Give me an example."

"The rest of the subject's immune system could consider the new cells a threat."

"You said it WORKS! What are you waiting for?" I demanded. "We are doing this and that's final!"

"It's pointless, Sir!" snapped Dr. Harrison. "We'd have to risk a patient's life to see the effects on a larger scale. This would be highly unethical. It's a miracle that the early tests even worked. I wasn't expecting it to be that easy, to be honest. Why don't we just leave it at that? Perhaps you could just present these papers to that Shadow Man of yours..."

"As vague as he is, the Shadow Man was very clear about the deal," I replied. "He wanted the cure to be successfully performed on a human body, and that's exactly what we're gonna do! Forget about ethics. We don't have time for those!"

"Forget about ethics? If you say that, you are never going to get another test subject. You know how much everyone mistrusts us after what happened to the previous patients!"

"No need to worry, Bill," I replied, scratching my chin. "I'm going to find my own test subject, and if you refuse to help with this project, I can fire you here and now!"

Bill slowly nodded.

"Very well... Sir," he sighed.

Although Dr. Harrison has told me the risks, I'm not backing out. This cure has got to work. I'll eat my tie if it doesn't! We didn't come this far just to stop in our tracks.

What is wrong with him? He has NO idea how much I'm going to pay him when we're done. With just fourteen days left, I don't have time to argue. I need to get my dollars from the Shadow Man, surprise the media, and best of all, get everybody to start trusting me again. Now all I need is a willing test subject.

Chapter 11

Kyle

When I got up this morning, I was thinking two things. First, we need a test subject, and second, Marty needs a new job. Both are priorities.

As for Dr. Harrison, he is still concerned about the safety of the treatment. His fellow scientists call it "unusual but seemingly practical." He is less optimistic.

I'm still confused. If the cure works on the cellular level, then why would using it on a patient's tumor be any different? Bill just can't see that. It doesn't matter. I decided to move forward myself and find a test subject, whether Bill likes it or not.

As for Marty, he has failed as a fast food cashier, a waiter, a railroad conductor, a worker in a nuclear power plant, a chef, and a janitor's assistant. I figured that if I wanted to keep a close watch on him, I should give him a position that has been empty for months: my assistant. Marty was very thrilled when I told him the news.

"Oh thank, you, Wilbur!" he said. "I won't let you down!"

Don't thank me yet, I thought. I decided not to call

Laurie immediately. I wanted to see if Marty would even remotely function as my assistant before making it official.

The first thing we did when we got to the office was grab the posters advertising our search for a test subject. We brought them out to the company van. I guess you could say I had a gut feeling that told me to drive out to Joe's Family Diner.

"Marty, today is going to be the day we find our next test subject," I declared.

The diner was all the way on the other side of town. We drove out of the neighborhood of small houses surrounding Helix Remedies. We then navigated through the industrial district, which Marty searched for trains. We eventually reached Main Street, and took it towards Downtown Juniper where the diner is located.

"Wilbur?" asked Marty. "If we find a test subject today, can I name him?"

"No, Marty," I replied. "We don't make up names. We'll be sticking to protocol. The test subject's name, male or female, will be Sigma."

"Oh yeah. Because Greek letters are cool," said Marty.

"That and the fact that Sigma is the eighteenth letter in the Greek alphabet, and this will be test subject number eighteen," I said.

"So why are we doing this search for a cancer cure thing again?" asked Marty. "I forgot."

"To get us ridiculously rich and to have everybody love us!" I replied.

"Don't you think we should be doing this for the good of humanity, rather than the company?"

"Yeah, humanity will have a nice page about us in the history books to read."

After I said that, Marty remained silent, which was unusual for him. I kept driving, and we passed some small shops before pulling into the dirt parking lot next to Joe's Family Diner. Marty and I hopped out of the car and went inside.

Joe's Family Diner has been a staple in Juniper for as long as I can remember. Joe and his brother, Sid, opened the place back in 1956. And it still looks like it did back then, I'm guessing. When you walk through the door, it's like stepping back in time.

There's an old jukebox by the door that still plays records. There are retro chairs, stools, booths, and neon and tin signs on the walls. There is a classic checkerboard floor. All the workers dress up in 50s styles and own 50s cars. The diner has authentic food, but not quite authentic prices.

I know everyone who works at this place. Back when my company was in its heyday, I preferred eating here to the fancy restaurants. Marty and I found a booth and sat down. I would soon figure out that finding a test subject was going to be easier than I had previously thought.

"What'll it be, Wilbur?" asked Beth, the waitress. She was wearing a light blue skirt and a white apron.

"I'll take my usual!" I replied.

"What about you?" she asked Marty, who had his nose buried in the menu.

"Me?" he replied. "I would like the burger meal with french fries and hash browns. Make it a kid's meal so I can get one of those toy cars!"

She stared at Marty with a look of confusion for a moment before writing down our orders. This always happens when Marty orders the kid's meal.

"The... kid's meal again?" questioned Beth. "Alrighty then! I'll have those meals over in just a jiffy!"

I asked Marty to go to the bulletin board and hang up one of the flyers. While I was waiting, I looked around at all the people in the diner. A woman with a baby was on the phone. A family with five noisy kids was seated nearby. How can the parents stay sane with that many children? Kids, yuck.

The one person who caught my eye the most was a grumpy-looking young man wearing a baseball cap and a shark tooth necklace. He also had hoop earrings in both ears. He was a contrast to all the noisy families, and seemed to singlehandedly drain all the excitement from the room. The young man and Beth were having a quiet conversation. Beth was well known by the townsfolk. Rather than visiting a counselor or psychiatrist, a lot of people went to her to discuss their problems. I couldn't help but listen in.

"They'll find a way, Kyle," said Beth. "Don't you worry!"

"They've tried everything!" snapped the guy. "I seriously doubt they'll find a cure."

The young man coughed several times in a row. It was a hacking cough. Kind of scary sounding.

"Why don't I just bring you a nice chocolate malt, free of charge? That'll cheer you right up!"

"Fine. It won't change anything though!"

Beth shook her head, and went back to the kitchen. I looked back at the guy. I could practically see steam rising from his head. He was obviously a very angry person.

Eventually, Beth came back from the kitchen with a tray and a malt. She set the malt down on the young man's table, and made her way over to where I was sitting.

"Alright Wilbur," said Beth, as she handed me the tray. "Here's a burger with fries and a root beer, and a kid's meal. Where's Marty?"

I looked around and saw Marty aimlessly wandering around the diner. "Oh," I replied, "he'll be back."

I suddenly heard a deafening growl followed by a crash. That angry guy had just shoved his malt off the table. The glass had shattered on the ground. Everybody in the restaurant stood up and stared in disbelief. You don't see that in public every day.

"What the heck is wrong with him?" I whispered to Beth. "Is he dying, or something?"

"Yes he is," she replied. "He has terminal lung cancer. How did you know?"

"I have to talk to him!" I gasped, struggling for air. It seemed everything was falling into place for me. I leaped out of my seat. When I turned I saw a look of confusion on Beth's face.

"I'll explain everything later!" I said frantically. I sprinted to Kyle's table, stepped over the shattered glass, and slid into the booth, sitting down next to him.

"What do you want?" Kyle groaned as he looked away, and slid as far away from me as he possibly could.

"I've heard that things haven't been going too well for you recently." That got his attention.

"Yeah?!" he growled. "You think?!"

"I can help you."

"Of course you can help me!" Kyle snapped. "By leaving me alone!" I wasn't surrendering yet. I decided to try a new approach. Combat sarcasm with sarcasm.

"Oh well," I sighed, as I slowly walked away, "I guess you'll just have to miss out on the amazing cure for cancer we've developed."

"Cure for cancer?" he snapped. "Who do you think you are?"

"Why, I'm Wilbur Watson. Founder, Owner, and CEO of Helix Remedies, The Greatest Place on Earth! Where dreams come true and miracles happen!"

"Isn't that Walt Disney World?" asked Kyle.

"I already told you," I continued, "I'm from Helix Remedies. We've developed a cure for cancer and you're the perfect candidate to try it out. I would like you to come to our facility."

"How do I know you're not going to fail me like all the other doctors have?!"

"Because no other doctors have seen our method."

"And what is this method?"

"Well... you'll just have to wait and see!"

"I've heard that line before. Not going to fall for it again. Forget it!"

"Fine, I'll just go ahead and tell you about the method then. Well, um… our scientists have discovered a cure for cancer in the DNA of a... previously undiscovered organism. They… extracted its DNA and watched it attack cancer cells and kill them."

I wished Dr. Harrison was there to explain how the cure works for me. I really didn't remember the details that well.

"Yeah right," replied Kyle.

"I swear to you it's true. How about you come to the lab with me and see the test results for yourself."

"Sure, why not. I don't have anything better to do this afternoon," sighed Kyle. "I was just planning to lie in bed, watch some TV, and continue suffering!"

"Well," I replied, "our facility is about twenty minutes from here. I'll give you the address."

"I don't have a car. I've been too busy lying in a hospital bed to learn how to drive. Heck, I don't even have a license or a learner's permit for that matter."

"That's okay. I'll drive you there. First, why don't we have lunch? I'll buy you a new malt."

Kyle didn't say anything so I assumed that was acceptable. A short time later, Beth wandered over and I ordered a new malt and a meal for Kyle. I invited him over to my table.

"Why are you doing this?" he asked, when his order arrived.

"I'm just trying to cheer you up," I replied. "Your suffering will be over soon!"

"I never said I was going to try your stupid cure," said

Kyle. He glared at me for a few seconds, then went on to devour his food. There was total silence. Once his plate was clean, we just sat there awkwardly staring at each other for a little while.

"Are you done eating?" I finally asked. "If so, why don't we head over to Helix."

"Yeah, I'm done," said Kyle, "and I've decided to go ahead and try out your cure. It better work though, or you'll be sorry you even existed."

The venom in his voice sent a slight chill down my spine, but I let it go. "Alrighty then," I exclaimed. "There will be just a few forms you need to sign when we get there, then we can begin curing you!"

Kyle reluctantly got up from the table and followed me towards the door. I stopped suddenly and turned around, looking for Marty. I nearly forgot I had brought him with. Just then, he came running towards us, carrying a take out box.

"Sir!" he said. "I couldn't find the bulletin board, so I went ahead and paid the bill. Here's the flyer."

"I don't need it," I replied. "We have our test subject."

"Test subject?" asked Kyle. "Isn't that the friendly way of saying 'lab rat'?"

"Who is this guy?" asked Marty.

"His name is Kyle. He's our new test subject and he's about to help save the company."

"Oh, hello. I'm Marty but you can call me Billy," he laughed. "Because I paid the bill!"

Marty started laughing uncontrollably. Apparently, because he had paid the bill, he thought it would be funny to pretend his name was Billy. Sometimes that kid really does say and do the strangest things.

"Marty, you've been a good assistant today. Thank you for taking care of that. I completely forgot about it."

Marty nodded and continued to laugh.

"Who are you laughing at?!" sneered Kyle.

"Ignore him," I whispered. "Now let's get to the van."

The white work van was easy to spot since it was one of the few vehicles in the parking lot that wasn't made in the 50s. It stuck out like a sore thumb. As we approached the van, I looked over at Kyle. He had a nervous look on his face. He was obviously a bit apprehensive.

"Sorry, but I'm not getting into a white van with a stranger. You could be a kidnapper or drug dealer," he said.

I ignored what he had said and responded, "It's not completely white. See? It says Helix on the door."

I suddenly noticed that the Helix Remedies logo on the door was very worn. "Just get in the van!" I demanded. "Wait that came out wrong. Let me try again. Please get into the vehicle, Kyle."

I motioned for Kyle to take the front seat on the passenger's side of the van. He hesitated at first, but after watching Marty excitedly leap into the back seat, he finally got in. Kyle turned and rolled his eyes at Marty, who was too busy to notice. He was already playing with the toy 50s car that came with the kid's meal.

I felt a sense of excitement as I pulled away from the diner. I had accomplished my goal for the day in record time. Not to mention, I took care of lunch too.

Chapter 12

Someplace Magical

<u>Saturday – Later</u>

We quickly pulled into the dusty parking lot outside Helix Remedies. A tall looming tower rose from the center of the main building.

"Where are we?" demanded Kyle, unbuckling his seatbelt. "You tricked me, didn't you?! That doesn't look like an office building. It looks like a hospital. I hate hospitals!"

"Where are we?" I replied enthusiastically. "We're someplace magical, and full of wonder!"

"Yeah, right," Kyle groaned.

Everyone got out of the van and we made our way to the lobby.

"Why is there plywood on the windows?" asked Kyle.

"The lobby-" replied Marty.

"-Is being remodeled," I interrupted. "Let's take the side door."

Kyle didn't seem to know about the recent problems we had been having and I had no intention of telling him about them. We walked to the side of the building. I opened the side door and led Marty and Kyle into the elevator room. I realized there wasn't any plywood blocking the view of the

65

torn up lobby, but thankfully, Kyle didn't notice. All three of us stepped inside the elevator, but then Marty suddenly jumped out.

"Wilbur, can I go talk to the construction workers again?" he asked.

"Sure," I replied, "go ahead. Just be back in my office later today to check in."

"Yes Sir," said Marty, saluting me.

The doors creaked shut, and the elevator slowly began to descend to the labs. After around thirty seconds, the elevator dinged, and the doors slid open. When we got out of the elevator, Kyle didn't seem too happy to see all the men and women in lab coats. He made it clear at the diner that he hated doctors.

"Follow me, Kyle. The office we want to go to is right down this hallway." Kyle followed me down the hall. I hoped he wasn't getting any second thoughts. I really needed to get this experiment underway.

I pulled open the door to the test subject office. Everyone inside was sitting around. A couple workers were nodding off. Because we haven't had any test subjects in the last few weeks, I've pretty much been paying these people to just sit at their desks. Luckily I hadn't fired them yet. There were still people around to sign Kyle up.

The Test Subject office is where candidates sign the official paperwork. They also meet with testing counselors, who make sure they are emotionally and mentally ready to participate in testing. The counselors explain the procedures and answer any questions people may have about the experiments they are going to be participating in.

"One new test subject. Hand me the latest form," I said to the man behind the counter. Kyle glared at the man, who was wearing a lab coat. As I've mentioned before, he doesn't like doctors.

"Does this young man need a testing counselor?" the man asked.

"That's me," I replied. "We have already discussed the cure. He just needs to sign the papers and get started."

"We hardly discussed anything!" snapped Kyle.

"Quiet," I responded. "He's just nervous. That's all."

"Sir, procedure is procedure!" demanded the man at the desk. "He will have to see a qualified testing counselor, and you are not one!"

"Oh fine," I replied with a sigh. "Do what you must."

The scientist hit a button and within a minute or two another man dressed in a lab coat came through the doorway.

"Hello Sir, who do we have here?" asked the counselor, whose name I believe is Fred.

"This is Kyle," I replied. "He has lung cancer and none of the treatments he has undergone so far have slowed it down. I have recruited him as a test subject for the cure we are working on and apparently I can't deal with the papers myself!"

"He looks a bit young," noticed Fred. "Do you have parental consent?"

"I'm eighteen," snapped Kyle. "I don't need a parent with me anymore."

"Well alrighty then Mister—" questioned Fred.

"Maxon. Kyle Maxon."

"Mr. Maxon, please follow me into my office and we'll get the paperwork signed.

We all stood up. I followed Fred and Kyle out the door of the waiting room and into Fred's office. As we sat down, Kyle looked nervous. He had started sweating and his eyes were darting back and forth.

"Let's just assume that the cure isn't going to work," he said. "What do I get for participating in your stupid study?"

"Well," I replied, "at the end of the test, you'll make

$100, plus you'll receive a lifetime supply of Helix Remedies brand products!"

"That would be a very small lifetime supply," Kyle replied darkly.

"Now, now son!" said Fred, shocked at Kyle's attitude. "Let's be positive! Now let me explain the procedures to you. The first thing we need to do is get a blood sample. That way the scientists can turn your white blood cells into superheroes!"

"You've gotta be kidding me," snapped Kyle. "Do I look like I'm 4? Superheroes, really? I've gone through honors biology."

"Right," Fred replied, "sorry about that. I was accidentally reading the introduction intended for child test subjects. Let me put it to you this way then. The scientists need a blood sample so they can not only reprogram your immune cells to target cancer, but also allow them to enter the tumor."

"So how many injections does this involve daily?" asked Kyle.

"Initially two a day so we can build up the number of modified white blood cells in your system," Fred explained.

Kyle groaned in response to hearing that.

"It shouldn't hurt too much," I replied, with a weak smile.

"Sir! According to your own rules, nobody can interfere with the test counseling experience!" demanded Fred.

"Yeah, this sure is an experience," sighed Kyle, rolling his eyes.

"Okay, Mr. Honors Biology," said Fred, grabbing a copy of the scientific paper Dr. Harrison had written about the cure. "Can you understand all this?" Kyle stared at the title of the report and cringed.

"Dr. Harrison's a bit cryptic in his papers," I replied, noticing his discomfort.

"Sir?" questioned Fred, clearly annoyed at this point. "Do you want to be thrown out?"

"You won't have to throw me out," I replied. "I'm leaving the room now. Bye."

I got up and left Fred's office and took my place in the waiting room where I planned to remain until Fred and Kyle were done. About a half hour later, they emerged from Fred's office. I was expecting Fred to at least acknowledge me, but he didn't say a word. He left and I assume returned to his office. I then led Kyle to the guest room he'd be staying in for a week.

We navigated through winding hallways filled with people in white coats. We then came to a door right across from the elevator and I took out a key.

"Ah," I said as I opened the door, "here we are. Here's where you'll be staying!" I flipped on the light switch. The room was filled with boxes, chemical tanks, and other junk. It was so small that I wouldn't have been able to lie down from one end of the room to the other.

"Wow," said Kyle. "Very nice. There's even a television in here."

"Oops," I replied, "this is a storage closet. Your actual bedroom is right over there." I unlocked the next door over.

"Here we go!" I said.

The hotel-sized room had warm lighting, but was filled with a musty smell. This place had not been used in a while. There was luxurious red carpet on the floor, a sofa, a captain's bed, and a wooden dresser. The room was complete with a dated television on a stand, and a restroom.

"This is for me?" asked Kyle with the slightest hint of excitement. "You've got to be joking."

"Celebrities used to stay in this very room back when we made hair products!"

"You sell hair products?"

"Not anymore," I replied, "but we still have some around. Want to try some?"

Kyle stared at me for a few seconds, then snapped, "Let's see if this cure works first."

"Don't worry," I replied. "The cure will work. Now remember, you aren't confined to the guest room. Feel free to grab a bite to eat in the mess hall and meet the scientists!"

"I don't want to meet anybody!" I ignored Kyle and continued to treat him like we used to treat the celebrity test subjects.

"That's okay," I replied cheerfully. "In the meantime, I've provided you with Helix Remedies shampoo and conditioner, a water jet comb, an eyebrow comb, shaving cream, a complimentary towel, and a-"

"Just leave me alone!" he hissed. Kyle slammed the door just an inch away from my nose. I turned around and saw that Dr. Harrison was right behind me, holding a clipboard.

"Who was that, Sir?!" he demanded. "You didn't actually go out and find a test subject did you?!"

"Oh yes I did, Bill!" I replied proudly. "You got a problem with that?"

"Why yes Sir I do!"

I ignored Bill's comment and continued, "His name is Kyle Maxon and I found him at the diner. He is dying of a terminal cancer and is desperate for a cure, which we just happen to have thanks to you!"

"The diner?!" snapped Dr. Harrison. "Somehow I knew you'd be dragging some poor soul into this! This scenario sounds awfully familiar, Wilbur!"

"Ah, don't be like that, Bill," I replied confidently. "We're only halfway back to fame and fortune. You said yourself this cure was gonna work."

"There are too many variables," snapped Dr. Harrison. "Do we really want to take the risk of killing someone? And how are we even going to get the tumor sample? I'm not a surgeon. And if Wayne wasn't on vacation right now, he probably wouldn't help you either!"

"I already have an idea. I happen to have a friend at the last hospital Kyle was at. I can ask him to secure a sample for me. He works in the lab and would be able to gain access to Kyle's tissue samples."

"I hope you know what you're doing Sir, because I sure don't!"

Dr. Harrison said to me himself last night that the cure would work. So why is he so concerned about it? Our cure for cancer will go exactly as planned, and that's final! I just know it will!

Chapter 13

Last Minute Jitters

<u>Sunday</u>

Its official. Kyle has signed up to participate in testing our new cure. The scientists have the tumor sample from the hospital and have talked Kyle into giving up some of his blood. They're busy preparing the cure for testing tomorrow. They have the DNA synthesizers fired up. I absolutely cannot wait for the first test of our most hopeful cure yet. It wasn't easy convincing Kyle to go through with all this though.

I expected our new test subject to be excited, roaming around the facility, and talking to the scientists; but I didn't see him the whole morning. After pouring through some spreadsheets, I decided to go look for him. The first place I looked was his guest room. I spotted Janitor Tom and Marty as I walked through the halls towards Kyle's room.

"Hello Sir," said Marty.

"What are you doing sweeping the floor?!" I asked enthusiastically. "You're my assistant now! Its official!"

Marty dropped his bucket and broom, spilling soapy water all over the floor. "How can I assist you, Wilbur!?" he replied, with excitement.

"First of all, clean up that mess. Second of all, get up to my office and alphabetize all the papers on my desk."

"I won't let you down!" he replied, running towards the elevator.

"Sorry about the mess, Tom," I said.

"That's okay Sir. I'll take care of it... as usual," Tom replied. "If you're looking for the test subject, he's not down here anymore. He went up to the lab to watch the scientists. I told him to be very careful."

"Thanks Tom," I said.

I went to the laboratory observation deck and that's where I found Kyle. He was sitting alone and watching the scientists do their work.

"Hi there," I said, pulling up a chair and sitting next to him. Kyle didn't respond.

"Hi there!" I exclaimed, this time a little louder.

Kyle turned around and sighed, "Oh hi. How long have you been sitting there?"

"Oh, about a minute," I replied. "I just got here,"

"Then that's a minute too long!" he said sternly. "Get out of my face!"

"No! This is my spot, and no kid is going to tell me I can't be here."

"I'm not a kid," said Kyle. "I may be younger than you, but I'm no kid."

"How old are you again?" I asked.

"I'm eighteen going on ninety."

"So how long have you had this cancer anyway?"

"I was diagnosed at age seven," he hissed. "I was actually sick for at least a year or two before that. I was in and out of hospitals so much that it interfered with school. I'm eighteen and still in eleventh grade. When I'm not in school, I'm hopping around the country searching for a better hospital than the last one. Every time I stepped into one of those hospitals, they told me they were going to help make me better, but most of the time I came out worse."

"Well, you've reached the end of your journey!" I exclaimed.

"You can drop the metaphors," snapped Kyle. "Of course I've reached the end of my life."

"I haven't finished my sentence. What I meant was that this will be your last disappointment!" Kyle stared at the scientists angrily and coughed violently a couple of times. "What wrong?" I asked.

"I'm dying," he said, when he finally stopped coughing. "If you had five months, maybe less to live, you'd realize how much of a problem that is."

"Then shouldn't you be happy to see the scientists hard at work?!" I asked. "They're soon gonna save you!"

"No they won't. They'll fail. I know from past experience." As I thought about what Kyle had just said, the group of scientists closest to the observation window started to laugh, and Kyle lost it. "STOP! LAUGHING! AT! ME!" he yelled. His scream was followed by a hacking cough. The scientists looked up for a second, but then got back to chatting.

"They're not laughing at you," I replied, "but I know how you feel. I sometimes think they're laughing at me when I come in here."

"I hate laughter!" interrupted Kyle. "It's a sign that everyone else is having more fun than me."

"And it's impossible to tell whether or not they're talking about me," I continued.

Kyle's eyebrow raised slightly. "You're sounding just like me," he said quietly.

"No, you're sounding just like me. I wish I could be more like Dr. Harrison," I continued. "He knows and has the respect of more people in the building than I do, and I run the place. It's good to hear I'm not the only one going through stuff like that. You're not alone. I'm alone too."

"Who is Dr. Harrison?" asked Kyle.

"My honorary ethics consultant," I replied sarcastically. "Actually Dr. Harrison is one of the scientists in charge of the search for a cure and everyone loves him. He has incredible ethics and he's such a brilliant guy. We wouldn't have discovered the cure without him."

"I want to meet this Dr. Harrison," said Kyle.

"I don't think he'll like you."

"Why not?" Kyle asked.

"Well, for one thing he doesn't like me, and he's not too thrilled that I allowed a test subject to come into the lab."

"Why is that?" I struggled to come up with an answer so I made one up. The last thing Kyle needed to hear is that the place has a bad reputation and a number of pending lawsuits against it.

"Uh, it has nothing to do with you," I lied. "It's just that he's very protective of his secrets." I figured a distraction was what it would take to prevent Kyle from chickening out. I really need this test to work! "You still don't think it'll work, do you?" I asked.

"Have I not made that clear?" replied Kyle.

"Have some faith, young man! We have discovered a cure for cancer practically out of nowhere, and it's going to finally put us on the map! Not to mention, it's going to save your life. It's a win for both of us!"

"Why should I care? I gave up on living a long time ago."

"When a huge opportunity lands in your lap, no matter how crazy, or risky, you should take it and work out the details later."

"So," Kyle sneered, "are you saying that being cured with your magic serum could be an opportunity I wouldn't want to miss?"

"You could say that," I replied. "Now, I don't want to see any last-minute jitters, kid. Are you positive you want to go through with this? There is no turning back you know, and we are not sure what's going to happen."

"On the off chance that this could work, sure, why not?" That was the answer we needed.

"Great!" I replied.

"I have to see counselor Jessica, but if she's anything like my school counselor, I'm not sure if I want to."

"If your school counselor can dig up your deepest darkest secrets, than you'd want to avoid ours. I'm giving you permission to skip that counseling session."

"Thanks," Kyle replied.

"Don't mention it," I said. "Please."

Chapter 14

The Injection

Today was the big day. We tested out the cure for the first time. There's no way to tell if it's working until tomorrow. I cannot wait.

I found out this morning that according to my own protocol, I apparently can no longer call test subjects by their real names. All of the scientists are insisting that I call Kyle "Subject Sigma" from now on. I wasn't sure if he'd react well to that.

After finishing my morning work, I made my way to Kyle's, I mean Sigma's, guest room. According to the scientists and doctors, he had been late for the experiment and I was sent to check on him. As I approached the door to the guest room, I thought about what I would say to reassure him. I was pretty sure that he was still nervous. I guess I had a gut feeling.

Unlike most days, the hallway wasn't quiet. Music was blaring from Sigma's room. I knocked on the door. There was no answer. I didn't bother to try again. I reached for my keys and opened the door.

Sigma was inside, sitting on the sofa in the corner of

the room. He was looking at his phone with his earbuds in. He wasn't wearing his baseball cap and I noticed that he actually had long hair.

"Test Subject?" I asked. I heard a grunt. That got his attention. When he heard me, he turned of the music and the area grew silent.

"You," he snapped, then coughed. "What are you doing here? Is privacy not a thing at this place?"

"Sorry, Sigma," I apologized, "but that noise was preventing you from hearing my knocks."

"It's not noise. Its metal! And who are you calling Sigma? Last time I checked, my name was Kyle!"

"Your name for the purpose of the experiment is Sigma," I replied. "The scientists have instructed me to call you that, so all the records will remain consistent."

"You're calling me Kyle, and that's final," said Sigma.

"We'll work on that later," I replied. "By the way, why's your hair long? I thought you had cancer?"

"I gave up on chemo long ago. My hair has been growing back ever since. I haven't cut it." I hoped what I brought would cheer him up a bit.

"I have something for you!" I exclaimed, handing him a picture frame.

"What's this thing?" he asked, taking it.

"This is an 8x10 picture of me!" I replied. "I had a few extra photos lying around, and every room in the building should have one."

"Gee, thanks a million. How come everything here is just crazy?" He dropped the frame on the end table face down.

"That hurts," I replied, not answering his question.

"Is this ALL you came here for?" Sigma sighed.

"No, Sigma," I replied. "I came because it's time to get the testing underway! Please follow me." Sigma remained on the couch. It didn't seem like he was going to budge.

I looked around. Sigma's belongings were scattered around the room. Clean clothes covered the dressers. Dirty clothes were piled up in the corner of the room. "Looks like you've settled in," I said, not expecting a reply. I was wrong.

"Yeah, I guess," sighed Sigma. "For a medical facility, it's not that bad. I've stayed in a lot of them, and this is actually one of the better ones."

"That's nice to hear," I replied. "The furniture's slightly dated and that's not changing anytime soon." Sigma didn't say anything.

"Well," I asked, "are you ready to head over to the lab now? We were supposed to be there an hour ago."

"I am not ready yet," said Sigma.

"I know that you're a bit nervous. To be honest, I'm just as anxious as you are, but it's time to get the experiment underway. Come on."

Sigma stood up, grabbed his baseball cap off the desk and put it on. "Alright," he sighed. "I guess I'm ready. Lead the way."

Sigma and I made our way down the hallway and headed towards the medical bay. The waiting room was empty except for one scientist staffing the desk. "This is Subject Sigma," I stated. "We're here for today's cancer cure test."

"Right down the hall in room D," he replied. "They've been waiting for you."

"Thanks."

We walked down a long corridor and made our way to Medical Room D. Inside the room, Dr. Harrison, Dr. Wagner and two other scientists were all chatting. "Finally," said Dr. Harrison impatiently.

"Hello Sir, nice to see you again!" said Dr. Wagner, trying to sound cheerful. "Thanks for sending me on that great vacation!"

"Don't mention it," I sighed.

"And thank you for bringing Sigma over. We were wondering when he'd arrive."

"Sorry we're a little late," I said. "Sigma was a bit nervous, but he's alright now. We're ready to get started."

"Oh good. Hopefully this is our last inconvenience," sighed Dr. Harrison. "Sigma, please have a seat."

Sigma sat on the cot in the back of the room and crossed his arms. "You guys are sure this is going to work, right?" he asked. Dr. Harrison looked like he was going to say something but didn't.

"You don't know whether or not this cure will work, now do you?"

"Of course it will, Sigma!" I interrupted. "Dr. Harrison over here told me so!"

"So you're Dr. Harrison," said Sigma, staring at the scientist.

"The one and only," Dr. Harrison groaned. He obviously wasn't thrilled to be finally testing out his far-fetched idea on a real test subject.

One of the scientists wheeled over a shiny metal cart. On top of it was a light blue tray containing a bottle of rubbing alcohol, a cotton ball, a syringe, and a small test tube.

"How much should I give him, Bill?" asked Dr. Wagner.

"We'll start with one-half-milliliter," replied Dr. Harrison. "Try to get it right on the line. Use a magnifying glass if you have to."

"Are you sure that's enough?" asked Sigma. "In the past I've received two or even three milliliters of medication at a time."

"Yes, it's enough."

Dr. Wagner reached for the syringe and extracted some of the cure from the bottle. "Roll up your sleeve, please," he said.

Sigma rolled up his sleeve, then another doctor rubbed a spot on his arm with a cotton ball that had been dipped in alcohol. "You know Sir," warned Dr. Harrison, "once we do this there's no turning back. You're going to have to accept and deal with whatever happens."

"I know. I know. Get on with it," I demanded.

Sigma stared at me, wondering what that odd exchange was all about. As Dr. Wagner moved the needle toward Sigma, his face turned white. He squeezed his eyes shut and grimaced when the needle went in. Once he was done, Dr. Wagner placed a Helix Remedies brand bandage over the injection spot.

"Okay," said Wayne. "All set. Let me know right away if you start feeling strange, which you shouldn't, but if you do, let me know. You can go back to your room now if you want. I don't need you back here until 7 p.m. when we need to do the next injection."

"Alright," Sigma sneered. "I can't wait."

"Would you like a soda or something, Sigma, for having to endure that?" I laughed.

"Sure, thanks," he sighed.

I dug into my pocket and pulled out a dollar. "Here you go. There's a soda machine right around the corner from the dentist office. See you later."

As Sigma made his way down the corridor, I was feeling very hopeful. If this works, Helix Remedies will be back in the headlines, only this time in a positive light.

Chapter 15

It's Working

<u>Wednesday</u>

Nothing much happened on Tuesday, so I decided to skip a day in my journal. The only time Sigma left his room yesterday was to get his food and two injections of the cure. I really wish that kid would show his face more.

I spent this morning pouring over spreadsheets, trying to see where I could trim the budget. So far, I see no way to restore Helix to its former glory until we get the money from the Shadow Man, and that can't happen soon enough.

I've often wondered who the Shadow Man really is and where the money is going to come from. Will he be handing me a check or a bunch of cash in a briefcase? Nah, he'll probably just have the money transferred into my bank account. I wonder if I'll be able to trace where that deposit came from when I do get it.

After looking through spreadsheets, I headed down to the medical bay to see if Sigma had gotten his blood drawn yet. The blood test was supposed to determine whether or not the cure is working. Sigma had received his fifth injection of the cure early this morning.

When I entered the exam room, the doctors were just

82

preparing to draw some of his blood. They first had to convince Sigma, who was wandering around the room, to sit down.

"Good morning Sigma!" I announced. "How's life?"

"Great, actually!" he sneered. "I'm dying of cancer, and because of all the needles, I can hardly feel my arms anymore!"

"Show a little bit of excitement!" I replied. "Today could be the day we make history."

He didn't say anything, but I swear a low rumble came from Sigma's throat. I remember thinking how strange that was. Perhaps he was just tired. As the nurse got ready to draw blood, she noticed a dark gray patch on his forearm. From where I was standing, it looked like a scab.

"What is that?" she asked.

"I don't know," replied Sigma. "It was there when I woke up this morning and it's extremely itchy."

"It could be a response from his immune system to the shots," said Dr. Wagner. "Why don't we change the injection site to his leg instead and see if there's an identical reaction. By the way, Wilbur, where is Dr. Harrison?"

"He's whipping up another batch of the cure in the lab," I replied.

"Oh that's nice," said Sigma. "I hope he remembers the flour."

"Very funny, young man," replied Dr. Wagner. "Now sit back down. We need that blood sample from you so we can see what kind of effect the cure is having on your body."

"Okay, just do it then," said Sigma, as he sat back down on the cot. The nurse came over, wiped a spot on Sigma's leg with alcohol, then withdrew the blood needed for the test. Once she had the vials labeled and bagged up she said, "I'm going to run these down to the lab. See you later."

After Sigma and the nurse left the room, I went back to my office to continue sifting through spreadsheets. After about twenty minutes, there was a knock at the door. It was Marty. "What do you want?" I asked. "There better not be another train you want to watch!"

"No Sir," said Marty." Doctors Wagner and Harrison are here to see you."

"Send them in," I said.

As the men walked into my office, they appeared deep in thought. "Who goes first?" asked Wayne.

"Not me," said Dr. Harrison. "You go ahead."

"No, Bill." I said. "You go first. I hope you brought good news."

"Alright Sir," replied Dr. Harrison. "The results from the blood tests and scans show that two percent of Subject Sigma's tumor has been neutralized. Because of the budget you provided for this project, we have very precise equipment with very small margins of error."

"Wait. What?"

"In layman's terms, the cure appears to be working."

"Appears?" I asked.

"In your terms, the cure is working," groaned Dr. Harrison. "Happy now?"

I was starting to see dollar signs everywhere, and couldn't wait to report the news to the Shadow Man. Of course one never knows when he is going to show up, and it has only been two days since the first injection. If we're lucky, the tumor will continue to shrink and maybe even be gone by Friday and I'd still have a week to spare until the Shadow Man's deadline. Heck, we could hold a public banquet on Sunday.

Wait a minute. Do I have room for that in the budget? It really doesn't matter does it? I can just fire a couple more people to pay for it and then hire them back later.

It will be a wonderful party. Reporters from all over the world will attend, and apologize to me for all the bad publicity they gave my company. Investors everywhere will be fighting with each other for a piece of the action. Dr. Harrison, Dr. Wagner, and Counselor Jessica will be sorry they ever doubted me. Finally, Helix Remedies will get the positive recognition it deserves.

Looks like this attempt at a cure is going to be our last one! Boy, this is the next big thing. Humanity will be forever proud of our breakthrough. Hopefully my name gets into the textbooks. My opposition will never know what hit it! Heck, humanity will never ever even know what hit it!

Chapter 16

The Sideshow Attraction

Thursday

When I walked into Medical Room D this morning, Sigma was sitting on the cot in the room with his shirt off. He was almost skeletally thin from his cancer. Just skin and bones. He was surrounded by scientists and doctors who were staring at him in disbelief; but not because of his physique.

I would soon realize that Sigma wasn't well at all. He had more of those gray scab-like patches on his body. Seemingly overnight, they had traveled from his arm to his chest, where they were a lighter shade. A few of the patches looked like they were under his skin. I'm also pretty sure that his fingernails weren't an inch long yesterday.

"Well," said Dr. Harrison to Dr. Wagner, "what do you make of this?"

"It still seems like it's an allergic reaction, but I've never seen anything like it before," Wayne replied. "Rashes are normally red. I have no idea why this one is gray. Normally it would take a burn to turn the skin gray and he hasn't been burned. The only other option is a fungal infection, but we definitely would have picked that up during Sigma's physical."

"And call me crazy, but it looks his skin is being replaced by the patches, rather than reacting to something," added a scientist whose name I couldn't remember. "It can't be due to allergies."

"Probably not," replied Wayne, "but there's no way to tell for sure until we obtain a sample and test it."

"Have you noticed that his fingernails have increased in length by two centimeters overnight?" asked Dr. Harrison. "That's another thing stumping me."

"Me too, Bill," replied Wayne. "Sigma? Has anything like this happened to you before?"

"No," Sigma exclaimed. "But maybe it's a sign I have TWO types of cancer now!"

"Let's note these in the logs as potential side effects of the cure," suggested another scientist.

"Agreed," said Wayne.

I was slightly troubled by the side effects Sigma was experiencing. I hoped they weren't permanent.

"How are you feeling today, Sigma?" I asked, before realizing that asking that question was probably a bad idea.

"My skin itches and it's turning gray," he snarled, rolling his eyes. "Plus I'm growing claws. I'm feeling GREAT today!"

"Don't worry, once your cancer is cured and we sort this out, you can return to your normal life!"

"Yes," replied Sigma. "My wonderful life. I'm eighteen years old and still live at home with my mommy and daddy. I haven't graduated from high school yet because I've missed too much of it. Cancer really sucks if you haven't realized that by now, and so does this cure. You never told me there would be side effects!

"Yes we did," I replied. "It says so right in the paperwork

you signed that there could be side effects, like this minor rash, for example."

"You call THIS a minor rash? You're turning me into a FREAK, you madman! If this continues, I'll be shipped to the circus as a sideshow attraction! They will call me Cattle Man."

"Don't worry Sigma," I reassured him. "I have no intention of shipping you off to Harvey's Happy Fun Fun Sideshow. And you won't look like this forever. I'm sure the great Dr. Harrison has a solution in mind, right Bill?"

"Not yet," said Dr. Harrison. "Before we can find a solution, we need to determine the cause."

"Then get to work on finding one, and do it quick if you want the weekend off," I suggested.

"Fine," he replied.

"Did you hear that? We're doing everything in our power to figure this side effect thing out and get you back to normal."

"You're telling the truth right?" asked Sigma.

"Of course. Have I ever lied to you?" I asked. Sigma didn't answer me.

"Alright," I said as I walked out the door. "This 'madman' has all the information he needs for today and will check in with you tomorrow."

I took the rest of the day off, while the scientists apparently spent hours talking Sigma into giving up a skin sample. From what I've heard, they never convinced him. They were, however, able to get a blood sample and concluded that Sigma's tumor had shrunk by another six percent.

With the good news comes bad though. This side effect is starting to look like a huge deal. Because of the many patches that had grown on his skin overnight, Sigma might just look like a sideshow attraction by the end of the week. But we can prevent that from happening, right? We've made it this far, have we not?

Chapter 17

Changes

Friday

It seems like I was just here, the medical bay, the place where miracles are made and dreams come true, or at least I used to think so. I poked my head into Sigma's usual examination room. The room was completely empty. The only light shining in was from the open doorway. There were no scientists, no doctors and no Sigma.

Suddenly I heard some frantic voices coming from down the hall in the Advanced Examination Room. I headed that way. When I cracked the door open, I was greeted with a terrifying sight. Sigma was on the ground being held down by two scientists. His arms were flailing and his legs were kicking. A third scientist was in the corner of the room with his nose bleeding and a few teeth missing.

"Is this a bad time, guys?" I asked.

"Thank goodness we're in a medical bay!" panicked Dr. Wagner. "Go to the examination room next door and I'll send somebody over immediately!"

The bleeding scientist got up, holding his hand out to catch the blood trickling down his face. He clumsily dragged the whole box of tissues off the counter. Dr. Harrison was in the room too, with a look of shock on his face.

"What in the name of medical progress is going on here?" I asked.

Dr. Wagner ran up to me. He had a frown on his face that showed no sign of good news. "Subject Sigma is experiencing more side effects," he whispered, "and we've never seen anything like them. Nobody has."

I watched as three scientists forced Sigma back onto the cot. When they were done, they immediately ran to the other side of the room.

"Its freezing in here!" Sigma hissed. "Can't any of you idiots turn up the heat?!"

"Your body temperature is a few degrees below normal," replied a scientist.

Wayne adjusted the thermostat by the doorway. I looked over at Sigma. He was more pale and skinny than before. His long black hair was gone except for a few strands hanging every which way. There were even more gray patches on his body. Most of them were on his chest and left arm, but there were also some on his back, and a few on his face. Most of them were now just under the surface of his skin. I walked towards Sigma out of curiosity. I looked closely at his skin and noticed that some of the patches were beginning to form oval patterns.

"What are you looking at?" Sigma growled.

"How are you feeling?" I asked.

"I feel fantastic!" he said with fake enthusiasm. "Can't you tell?" I circled around him like a vulture.

"Curious," I whispered, as I reached toward his back. "Curious. If I didn't know better I'd think those were-"

"GET YOUR HANDS AWAY FROM ME!" snarled Sigma, his voice full of venom. I pulled my hand away and then ran back to where Dr. Wagner was standing.

"Let's talk outside," I said. Doctors Wagner and Harrison nodded and we left the room. Two security guards rushed inside.

"Okay," I said. "Any idea what's happening to our test subject?"

"I'm certain that whatever is happening isn't an allergic reaction," Wayne replied. "He has these plate-like growths all over his skin. His fingernails are an inch-and-a-half long, and he's getting increasingly aggressive. There have probably been more changes too, but he won't let us examine him or obtain a blood or tissue sample. There's also no way of knowing if his cancer count has gone down. And I have no idea how all of these changes could be happening this fast. It's just not naturally possible."

"Until we get some sort of tissue sample there aren't going to be any answers," said Dr. Harrison. "Sigma has already injured three scientists this morning. I recommend we sedate him. That way we can examine him safely."

"I don't think he'd like that very much," I said.

"Alright, Sir," replied Dr. Harrison, "I think we should at least postpone today's injections until we figure out if the cure and these anomalies are related."

"Good idea, Bill," I said.

"Agreed," said Dr. Wagner.

I looked through the window and spotted Sigma with his nose towards the ceiling.

"Just what the heck is he doing?" asked Dr. Harrison.

"Let's go back inside and see," I said.

Dr. Harrison cautiously opened the door a crack. Sigma looked over briefly, then got back to what he was doing. There was a fly buzzing around the light fixture above. Sigma reached up and slapped the light with a thud, and the fly fell to the floor. He then reached down, snatched it up, and put it in his mouth.

"YUM!" hissed Sigma, laughing wildly as he looked at us. "I never thought bugs could be so satisfying!"

"I think I'm going to be sick," I said, feeling a bit lightheaded.

The two scientists in the room looked at each other and shrugged. They stared at Sigma with confusion as they jotted down vigorous notes.

"Okay… Sigma," I stuttered. "I think you're free to go back to your room for the day." He looked up, wrinkled his nose as if sniffing the air.

"Sigma?" I asked. "Are you coming?"

Sigma grunted in response. He then put his shirt and baseball cap back on and followed me out of the examination room without a word. Dr. Harrison was right. Something has gone wrong with the cure. But what? This test may be going somewhere, but it isn't going well.

Chapter 18

Transformation

Normally I take weekends off, but because of what's been happening with Sigma I thought it would be a good idea to come to work today. When I went downstairs to check on Sigma, I noticed that a group of scientists and security guards were trying to gain entrance to his room. They were knocking very loudly, but not getting any response. Among them were Dr. Wagner and Dr. Harrison.

"What seems to be the problem?" I asked.

"Our night guard said that he heard ear piercing screams coming from here," said Dr. Wagner. "We know Sigma is in there but he's not answering the door."

"I'll just let myself in," I said.

"Sir?" questioned Dr. Harrison. "I don't think that's a good idea."

I ignored him, pulled out my giant key chain and found the key. I put it in the lock and turned it, and cautiously opened the door. Dr. Wagner and I entered the room, which was pitch black. A security guard came over and turned on his flashlight. When I caught my first glimpse of the room, my jaw dropped.

Everything in there had been completely torn to shreds. There were scraps of fabric and feathers from the bed everywhere. There were scratch marks on the sofa, and the TV was smashed. I could hear something breathing heavily in the room. Then the guard shined the flashlight in the direction of the breathing. It was Sigma. He looked plain awful. Wait a minute. Awful doesn't even begin to describe the chilling sight I saw.

Sigma was huddled in the corner, completely naked, except for his shark tooth necklace and earrings. There were pieces of his clothing scattered about the room. Sigma looked like he was in pain. He was drenched with sweat, shivering and breathing heavily. Thick purple veins bulged from his face.

His skin was almost completely covered in small, dark gray oval plates. The plates on his chest and throat were a lighter color than those on his back and sides. Imagine being covered in blisters. Next, imagine your worst sunburn. Add the two together, and multiply by ten. That's what Sigma's skin looked like to me.

The plates on his body closely resembled the scales of a snake or lizard. The nails on his hands and feet had blackened and were over two inches long. I then looked at Sigma's eyes. I'll never forget those eyes. His irises were now red with slitted pupils. And they were staring right at me. I was hit with a wave of uncontrollable shivering. We all were.

"What the-?" I asked. "What the heck happened to Sigma?"

"I-it appears that Sigma has undergone more… changes overnight," stuttered Wayne. "That must be why Officer Jones over here heard that… dreadful screaming."

"What are we going to do?" I asked.

"I recommend we put Sigma in a containment chamber for his own safety."

"And our safety too?" I asked.

"Yes," replied Dr. Wagner. "If one of us had been in the room overnight, this could have been a murder scene. Once we set up the chamber, all contact with Sigma must involve teams of two or more. And precautions must be taken before entering the chamber."

"YOU," growled a deep voice. It was Sigma, who had finally decided to speak. He pointed at me with a long clawed finger. "WHAT ARE YOU DOING TO MY BODY?!"

His voice echoed throughout the room, sending another shiver up my spine. "Calm down, Sigma," I said. "Please. We're gonna help you."

"BY CAGING ME UP LIKE AN ANIMAL?" he roared. "I DON'T THINK SO!"

"I don't know about you guys, but now would probably be a good time to sedate him," suggested Dr. Harrison.

Sigma put a clawed hand on the wall and tried to get up.

"YOU LIED TO ME!" he snarled. "YOU NEVER TOLD ME THIS WOULD HAPPEN!"

I signaled the security guard to tranquilize Sigma. The guard pulled the trigger and a dart instantly stuck into his scaly arm. Before long, Sigma tumbled back to the ground and slumped over against the wall. Two guards came over and lifted him up. They carried him onto a cot, which they wheeled away.

"What," I stuttered. "What are we going to do?"

"I don't know Sir," said Dr. Wagner. "I don't know."

"Dr. Harrison?" I asked. "Is this what you meant by potential side effects?"

"No Sir," he replied. "This is not what I meant."

I was certain at that moment that my dreams were over. Rather than becoming rich and famous again, I was suddenly in the middle of my worst nightmare. It was obvious in my mind that some kind of transformation was underway, but what? Just what was Sigma becoming?

Chapter 19

Reptilian

<u>Sunday</u>

As I walked down to the containment chamber this morning, all kinds of things were going through my mind, which these days is a pretty busy place. What would Sigma be doing? Would he still be passed out? Would he be banging on the walls and shouting, like crazy people do in the movies?

There was a security guard posted by the door to the containment chamber. When he noticed me, he stepped aside to let me in. I arrived to find a large window overlooking a room that had nothing in it but a toilet, a shower head, a metal cot, and large white tiles on the walls, floor, and ceiling. There was a team of scientists sitting at a long desk by the window. They were all taking vigorous notes.

This part of the building used to house the psychiatric ward for Juniper General Hospital. There is an entire hallway lined with rooms just like this one. They're quite handy when test subjects become irrational, aggressive, or otherwise need to be contained.

I spotted Sigma sitting in the corner. He was still naked. I thought the scientists would have given him a new set of clothes by now, but they hadn't. Sigma didn't look dangerous at the moment, but based on what happened yesterday he could lose it again at any time. The safest place for him—and us—is definitely the containment chamber where he is now staying.

Suddenly, Sigma looked up and glared at me with his new set of red eyes. I observed that aside from a few patches of remaining human skin, his thin body was now completely covered in gray scales. They were mostly a dark gray, but there were lighter ones on the front of his body. There were also lighter scales on his forearms and feet that looked like gloves and socks.

"You!" he hissed in my direction, when he noticed me staring. His voice sounded even deeper than yesterday. "You can drop the charade. Is THIS what you really wanted a test subject for?"

I didn't know what to say so I remained silent. Sigma stood up and started coming towards me. I may have been standing behind a one inch thick glass pane, but I was downright terrified. I took a few steps back. As he got closer to the window, I noticed that his hands and feet were covered in larger scales, resembling the plates on bird legs. It was out of place to see that on human legs.

The only trace left of Sigma's humanity was the shape of his face, but even it was covered with scales. I couldn't stand looking at him for too long. I quickly directed my attention back to the scientists.

"What's happening to him?" I asked to nobody in particular. "What's he turning into?"

Dr. Wagner walked up to me. "I already told you this," said Wayne, "but I'll say it again. It's like nothing I've ever seen. He should be dead by now. His cells are dividing much faster than normal, and I don't know what they're turning him into. His metabolism is off the charts. He requested that one of us bring him five burgers from Joe's Family Diner this morning. I can't even eat one of those things, much less five. They're almost completely made of saturated fats!"

"Well, what does that mean? Does his body need more energy to change?"

"That's what we're assuming, but again Sir, we have no idea what's going on."

"Any vague idea?" I asked.

"From the looks of it," Wayne continued. "He may be turning into some kind of lizard."

"Lizard?" growled the voice of Sigma. "That's what I was thinking. Now bring me a rock and a heat lamp. It's freezing in here!"

"And he now has amazing hearing," said Wayne. "We aren't even using the microphone. He can hear us through the glass."

"And while you're at it," Sigma hissed, "some clothes and a shower curtain would be nice too! I'm starting to think privacy doesn't exist here! And by the way, stop looking at me while I'm changing!"

"Maybe Sigma knows something about all this that we don't," I suggested.

"Perhaps he does. Why don't we ask him," said Wayne. "Sigma, is there anything we don't know about you that could help us determine the cause of your transformation?"

"I'm not hiding anything," growled Sigma in response. "I am still NAKED, after all!"

"There's your answer, Sir." I looked behind me and saw two scientists wheeling in a Helix Remedies portable x-ray machine. They were accompanied by a security guard and Dr. Harrison.

"Doctor Wagner," said one of the scientists, "we're ready to begin the x-ray scan."

"Assuming we can get Sigma to cooperate," replied Wayne.

"Cooperate with WHAT?" growled Sigma.

"Just a simple x-ray scan," he replied. Before Sigma could say anything else, the guard opened the door of the containment chamber slightly and fired a tranquilizer dart into his leg.

"WHAT THE-?" asked Sigma as he drifted off and closed his eyes.

"Was that really necessary?" I asked. "He might have said yes."

"We don't know that, Sir," replied Dr. Harrison. "And this is a race against time. We need to find out what is going on as soon as possible."

It took the scientists half an hour to get all the scans they wanted. Sigma slept through the whole thing. While they were at it, they got tissue and blood samples. When they were done, two people wheeled the machine to the radiology room, while a scientist took the blood and tissue samples to the lab.

"How long do I have to wait?" I asked.

"Dr. Harrison and I are going to Radiology right now to see the scans," Wayne replied. "Why don't you come with us."

I followed them to the Radiology lab. In the room, numerous scientists were looming over a large screen in the center of the room on a table. They were going on and on about vertebrae and appendages.

"Can I take a look, guys?" I asked.

"Sure, Sir." said one of them, stepping away. On the table was a 3D scan of Sigma's skeleton. Upon closer examination, it did not look human. There were long claws on his hands and feet. I touched the screen and turned the image around. It looked like his backbone was expanding. Maybe it was forming... a tail? This all seemed dreadfully familiar. At first I couldn't place it, but then I realized it.

"Wait a minute!" I shouted.

"What?" asked one of the scientists.

"Bring up the scan you took of that skeleton we found in the tunnel and put it next to Sigma's x-ray." The scientist did as I asked and a second image appeared next to Sigma's. It had sharp claws, and a tail.

"No," I whispered.

There was no denying it. Sigma was turning into the creature we found in the tunnel. The same creature the cure came from. "Oh my God," I said in utter shock. "Sigma is turning into the creature. And it's… all.."

"I think you're right," said Dr. Harrison. "And it's ALL your fault. Now what are you going to do about it?"

"Me?" I asked. "You're the scientist."

"And you're the man who got us into this mess in the first place!"

Dr. Harrison angrily stormed out of the room and slammed the door. The picture of me on the wall crashed to the floor. The glass on the frame shattered as did my hopes for ever saving the company.

Janitor Tom was right. That creature is causing nothing but trouble. I can't believe that this is happening to me. What did I ever do to deserve this? I don't want to go to work tomorrow.

Chapter 20

When You Look Inside Them

Monday

Mondays at work are never a good thing, particularly when you have something as dramatic as Sigma's transformation going on. I really wish I didn't have to come to work today, but I did, so I decided to make the best of it.

Nothing could compare to the atmosphere at Helix today. Everyone's obviously terrified by what's happening to Sigma, but nobody can possibly understand how the whole thing is affecting me. I'm scared too. Really scared. Not to mention, I'm one hundred percent sure this all my fault.

The halls were silent except for nervous whispers. I felt like my entire staff was staring at me with suspicion. Nobody would dare greet me, for I was the one who wanted to look in the skeleton for a cure. It was I who caused this chain of events. The irony is that we created a working cure. Sigma's cancer is down by seventeen percent, but because of what's happening to him, that's almost meaningless.

I wish I could understand how this transformation could possibly be happening. Is it a curse? Some kind of dark sorcery? Is it the Shadow Man trying to send me a message? No, he wouldn't have wanted the cure to fail. Or was it Dr. Wagner and Dr. Harrison trying to get even? It might be possible.

I don't know if I'll ever have the answer. For now, I need to focus on what's happening to Sigma rather than why. At first I was reluctant to see him, but I was just too curious about how his condition had progressed to not go. When I got to the containment room, I knocked on the door.

"It's me, Wilbur," I said. "Let me in!"

A guard opened the door and let me inside, but didn't say a word. Dr. Wagner, Counselor Jessica, and a couple of scientists and guards were inside. Jessica was probably there to diagnose Sigma's descent into insanity, like she attempted to do with me.

"Good morning, Sir," said Dr. Wagner.

"Good morning?" I asked. "Glad you think so. Can I speak with Sigma?"

"Well…"

"I wouldn't recommend it, Sir," interrupted Counselor Jessica. "Sigma is aware of his surroundings, but his personality has become unpredictable."

"Unpredictable?"

"One minute, he's on his best behavior, then the next, he's threatening to tear someone's eyes out."

"There's also a new development in the transformation," added Wayne. "Sigma is growing a tail and it must be painful because he keeps going on and on about it."

"I still want to see him."

"Right this way then," said Wayne. "Follow me."

Sigma was sitting in the corner looking at his new tail that had appeared overnight. I also noticed that he was starting to grow black quill-like spines. They had emerged from his skull, backbone, arms, and chest. There was a strange bony growth on his nose. As for the tail, it was probably a foot long and it had come out from his tailbone.

"I have a TAIL?" Sigma hissed. "WHEN did this happen? HOW did this happen?"

"Again, we're not sure, Sigma," sighed Dr. Wagner.

"Well I don't want it! Make it go away!"

"I wish we could," Wayne whispered.

"And why are there spines on my spine?" Sigma hissed. He stood up and I took a few steps back, afraid he was going to leap towards the window.

"Please don't worry Sigma," I said. "We're doing everything in our power to reverse the transformation."

"Yeah, right! If you're the one who's transforming me, why would you want to TURN ME BACK?!"

Sigma leaped at the glass and snarled. In his open mouth were razor sharp teeth and a purple, forked tongue. I stepped back, and almost tripped over my own feet. Wayne caught me.

"I'm sorry I frightened you," said Sigma, smiling, showing off his new fangs. "I shouldn't have. You're doing all you can to save me and I trust that you will. JUST KIDDING! YOU'RE GOING TO FAIL!"

Sigma's voice seemed to thunder through the room. I realized that coming here was a bad idea.

"You were right, Counselor," I said, "I don't think there's anything I can do here. I'm going to my office."

"Would you like to talk about what's going on, Wilbur?" she asked.

"No thanks."

I had no time for a counseling session, particularly at a time like this. As I started to leave the room, Sigma spoke again.

"That day we talked at the balcony, I thought maybe you could become my friend," Sigma sneered. "For that one single day, I looked up to you. But now you seem so small. So insignificant. So useless."

"That hurts, Sigma," I replied. "Look, everything is going to be fine, but you've got to hang on just for a little longer."

"You don't know how many people have told me that and haven't kept their word."

I felt the urge to reassure Sigma some more, but knowing it wouldn't work, I just left the room. When I got back to my office, I picked up the phone and called Laurie.

"Laurie," I said into the receiver, "is the senior staff all here today?"

"Yes Sir," she replied. "Why do you ask? Does it have something to do with Sigma?"

"Yes. It's about time we hold an emergency meeting. Make sure Janitor Tom comes."

"Janitor Tom?" she questioned.

"Yes," I replied. "Please don't ask why."

"Yes, Sir."

A few hours later, I was at the head of the table in the conference room playing with my coffee mug. "Folks," I began, "I've asked you all to come here to update you on the cancer cure project. As many of you have heard, the cure appears to be working, but Subject Sigma is suffering from an unexpected side effect. He appears to be transforming. To what end, we're not sure."

"Transformation?" asked Marty. "What's he turning into? I wanna see!"

"No, Marty," I said. "You don't want to see it. I thought you were supposed to be in my office filing papers."

"But-"

"No buts, Marty. Now go back to my office and get to work."

He looked down and frowned before leaving the room. My way of handling Marty's request was kind of rude, but

I did not want to expose him to the horror of what was happening. He's just way too innocent.

"Sorry about that guys," I said. "Now let's get this meeting underway. I want to hear everyone's ideas. Tom? What do you know about what's happening to Sigma?"

"Well, like I said," he replied, "they're nothing but trouble. They kill, they maim, and they have no regard for-"

"Tell me something I don't know. How many of them are there? Where did they come from? And please explain how it's even possible for Sigma to be turning into one of them!"

"I don't know, I don't know, and I don't know."

"What do you know then?"

"I know that you should have listened to me, kid. I told you not to mess with the skeleton, and because of you, we're all going to die."

"I certainly hope not," I sighed. "Do you have any useful advice?"

"I say destroy that creature! That is the only solution!"

"I hear you Tom," I replied, "but that young man down there doesn't deserve to die just because you said so. We have to try and save him, and the first step is to figure out what is happening and why. I need ideas!"

"Well Sir," said Dr. Harrison, "the key to reversing the transformation is to find the cause. We need to find part of him that is still human and monitor it."

"As far as I can tell," I replied, "there's no humanity left."

"We're not certain of that. If we act fast, we might be able to find some tissue that hasn't transformed yet."

"How are we going to do that?" asked Wayne. "We can't just throw samples in the sequencing farm. It would take too long to get results."

"By the time the results come back," I added, "Sigma might be somebody's pet lizard."

"We need to find a more reliable way," said Dr. Harrison.

"Something that's easy to isolate."

"I know!" I said. "The tumor!"

"He's right!" said Dr. Wagner.

"Why yes he is," Dr. Harrison sighed. "We've been using the blood tests to see how much of Sigma's tumor has dissipated. We know for sure there's eighty-three percent left. That means eighty-three percent of it is made up of human cells. We have to surgically remove his lung tumor."

"Sigma isn't going to like that at all," I replied.

Bill and Wayne whispered to each other for a few seconds.

"Sir," announced Dr. Harrison. "We don't have much of a choice anymore. Wayne and I are going to prep for surgery."

"Alright," I replied, "fine."

"They don't like it when you look inside them," whispered Janitor Tom.

Chapter 21

Sleuthing

Tuesday

This morning's lab report called Sigma's surgery yesterday a success, but I don't consider it one. When he was told his lung tumor needed to be removed, Sigma lashed out and scratched a scientist in the face. After the attack, security rushed into the containment chamber to rescue the bleeding scientist and subdue Sigma. The scientist was rushed to the hospital for treatment. I'm told he required numerous stitches; and that it took two tranquilizer darts to knock Sigma out this time.

Once Sigma was under, Dr. Wagner's team successfully removed the tumor, and the scientists are in the lab searching for what could have possibly caused the transformation. Meantime, Sigma's situation hasn't gotten any better. The transformation continues. His tail and spines have grown longer, and from what I found out today, it's about to get worse.

I've been suspicious of everyone around here lately and decided this was the day I was going to do a little sleuthing. During the lunch hour, when everyone had cleared out of the lab, I decided the time had come to search Dr. Wagner's office to see what I could find. I looked behind me to make sure nobody was coming, and slipped inside.

First, I looked in all the drawers. I wasn't sure what I was looking for exactly, but thought maybe bank statements or notes about a hostile takeover would turn up. I didn't find anything of the sort. Just a few love letters from his wife and drawings from his kids. Kids, yuck. I also searched his closet. I found several matching lab coats and a straw hat that I couldn't imagine on Wayne's head. There was nothing to suggest that Wayne was plotting against me. But perhaps he would've expected me to look here.

Having found nothing, I carefully closed the door and made my way to Dr. Harrison's office across the hall. If anyone had something bad to say about me, it was him. I strongly believe that Dr. Harrison has been trying to kick me out of my company ever since we started the search for a cancer cure. He has made his opinions clear every time we brought in a new test subject. He doesn't approve of my methods. He supports animal testing (He's a monster!), and really doesn't like me in general. That's okay. I don't like him either.

While searching through his office, I found his journal and there was a very disturbing entry about myself. Apparently, Dr. Harrison thinks I'm unethical, and wants me arrested for what's happening to Sigma. I also found a copy of last year's staff yearbook. Everyone I've fired had their faces crossed out with permanent marker. Good to know I can't trust him either. He is good friends with Wayne, so I assume they're working together.

Disappointed that there was no concrete proof of a takeover, I decided to get back to work on the mountains of paperwork waiting for me. On my way, I stopped off at Janitor Tom's office. I checked the time. Lunch was still being served, and he typically hangs around the cafeteria until lunch is over. I think he likes one of the lunch ladies. Or maybe he's just there because it's his job to clean things up.

I knocked at the door and got no answer. I took out my key chain and let myself in. Janitor Tom's office was dimly lit and a mess as usual. The lights above hummed and flickered.

First, I decided to check the file cabinet. It was locked, as expected. Janitor Tom has always been very secretive. But I don't think he's very bright. I was certain the key was in an obvious place. I looked under his pencil sharpener, and sure enough, there was a key. I grabbed it, and tried it in the lock. It fit inside, and I smiled, but when I tried to turn it, my smile turned into a frown.

"Come on!" I yelled, shaking the file cabinet. "Open up!" Wrong key. Nervously looking at the clock, I saw that it was 12:26. I had to pick up my pace. I started looking under papers on his desk, eventually brushing a few onto the floor.

"Great," I whispered. I put them back, then opened the desk drawer. There was nothing interesting in there. Just love letters from his wife. Nobody ever wrote me a love letter. I angrily slammed the drawer. As I was trying to stand up, I noticed that my tie was caught in the drawer. I tried to pull it loose, but then gave up and opened the drawer. The clock read 12:31.

Next, I dropped to the floor, hoping to see something taped under his desk. There was a piece of gum, but no key. I can't believe Tom, a janitor, put gum under his desk. That's just wrong. Obviously, I was distracted by that horror. As I stood up, I banged my head on the edge of the desk.

"Ouch!" I yelled. "That hurt!"

I lost my balance, and fell backwards onto the chair. I reached under the seat to pull myself up, and felt something cold and metal. It was a key.

"Yes!" I exclaimed, ripping the tape from the bottom of the

chair. My head was throbbing at this point, but I ignored it. Instead, I tested out the key and it worked.

The first drawer was filled with gum wrappers. A few spilled out. There must have been hundreds of them in there. Some of them looked very old. Well, he has been here for a long time. Guess that makes sense. The second drawer is where he kept his time sheets. I looked through a few of the folders, and found sheets dating back to the 1960s. The third drawer was empty except for a few film negatives in a yellowing envelope labeled "Creature Examination, 1962". This is what I was looking for. I was sure of it.

I held one of the negatives up to the light, and saw what looked like two men in lab coats holding something down on a metal table. I couldn't tell what it was, because part of the film had been burned off. One of the men resembled Janitor Tom. I picked up another negative and was horrified by what I saw. It looked like an autopsy, but I couldn't tell on what. I put the negatives back in the envelope, and closed the drawer with my hands shaking.

I slowly pulled open the fourth and final drawer, the largest one in the file cabinet. Inside was something white in color with gray pieces on it. At first, it appeared to be a dyed cow skull, but I quickly realized what it really was. I had located the missing skull from the skeleton found in the tunnel. It had four horns on the back of its head. There was a spiked, bony plate on the snout. There were also spines sticking out of the top of the skull, the jaw, and the back. The skull's mouth was lined with fangs. Some of them were an inch long. The spines and fangs made me think of Sigma. Was this what his head was going to look like?

"You shouldn't have come here, Wilbur," said a voice behind me. I jumped. It was Janitor Tom. I quickly closed the drawer, and turned around.

"Hi Tom!" I laughed, trying to sound as if nothing had

happened. "Just looking around. I am, after all, the CEO of this company, heh heh!"

"That may be the case, but it doesn't give you the right to come into my office uninvited."

The next few seconds of awkward silence felt like hours.

"Find what you were looking for?"

I started trembling. He knew why I was here.

"Y-yes," I stuttered. "I believe I did. Care to explain?"

"No," Tom said quickly.

"Care to tell me what I just found in your drawer?"

"You know enough already."

"Tom, You owe me an explanation!"

"Wilbur," said Tom abruptly. "I have been sworn to secrecy."

"We have a kid in our medical wing who I think is turning into one of those things. Can't you make an exception?"

Tom looked down, and held his head.

"As I've told you, I can not reveal what happened in 1962. What I can tell you is that there's nothing we can do for that kid, but put him out of his misery. Those aliens are nothing but-"

"Aliens?" I asked.

"Creatures," said Tom. "I meant to say creatures."

"But you said aliens!" Tom ignored me and continued talking.

"Something terrible happened years ago, and because of what you're doing, it's about to happen again. If only all of the creatures had been destroyed as I thought they had."

"But one ended up in the tunnel, didn't it?"

"Yes. When I first heard the tunnels were going to be excavated, I was curious. When the construction team took a break after their first day, I snuck in and much to my horror discovered the skeleton."

"You found the skeleton before the rest of us did? And you took the skull?"

"Yes. I hid the skull, so you wouldn't suspect that the skeleton wasn't human. I was wrong. Not only did I forget to hide the tail, I forgot how much technology has advanced since my day. You kids and your fancy gadgets… You found out right away that the skeleton wasn't human. I tried to warn you about the creature over and over, but you didn't listen. Now that test subject of yours will probably kill you and everyone else in this building."

"Kill us?" I asked.

"Take one good look at that skull and you'll see it's evil. All I can tell you is to prepare for the worst. If that kid gets out, our lives will be in danger. Your company will be in danger more so than it is now."

"So what do you recommend I do?"

"Didn't you hear me, kid? Put him out of his misery. Kill him and burn the remains. You should burn this skull and the skeleton too. We can't allow history to repeat itself."

My heart was pounding as I absorbed what Tom had just told me. I was thinking two things at that point. Janitor Tom is insane and we're in big trouble.

"Tom," I demanded, "we don't kill anybody at Helix. Well at least not intentionally. Nothing bad is going to happen to Sigma! You hear me? Nothing! Stay away from him!"

I stormed out of Tom's office and he followed me. "Wait Wilbur! There is something I have been meaning to ask you. Can you describe this Shadow Man of yours?"

"I will not! He is none of your business!"

I turned away and started walking back to my office. Much to my relief, Tom didn't follow me. As I walked down the corridor, a million questions were going through my mind. Why is Tom all of a sudden interested in the Shadow Man? Why does he want to destroy the skeleton we found and Sigma? I didn't care what that crazy old man had to say. We're going to save Sigma.

Chapter 22

Pointing Fingers

<u>Wednesday</u>

This morning, I pulled into the parking space next to a dumpster. The damaged Helix Remedies logo from the lobby was still sticking out. I got out of my car and shook my head in disgust.

I entered the building through the plywood door to the boarded up lobby. If we had anything that resembled a balanced budget, it would probably be repaired by now. Repairs were going slowly. The concrete floor was looking a little better, but the walls were still a mess. You'd think they'd start with the walls rather than the floor. There are still some nasty messages to yours truly on them. They should have been gone a week ago. I'll have to tell Laurie to yell at the contractors.

My plan was to head to my office, but I was distracted by a commotion in the security room by the lobby. "Just look at him!" snapped Dr. Harrison. "He has some nerve to be going through my office like that!"

"What does he think he's doing?" yelled Wayne.

"Now gentlemen," said a security officer. "Calm down. No need to worry or get upset. We'll get to the bottom of this when Wilbur gets into the office. I'm sure he'll have an explanation for this."

I peeked through the window and saw a guard, Dr. Wagner, Dr. Harrison, Janitor Tom, and a scientist with his arm in a sling gathered around the security station. This scientist in particular had been injured by Sigma. I ran to the doorway. "You called?" I asked smiling. "Are you watching the video of the time I fell in the company pool again?"

"You know fully well what we're watching," said Dr. Harrison. "Care to explain?"

"Nope," I said.

"Well Sir," said the security officer, "you owe them an explanation. Clearly that's you in their offices searching their drawers during yesterday's lunch hour."

"Fine," I sighed, "I was trying to make sure that my company was secure. There have been a lot of strange things going on lately, like a particular transformation?!"

"Well, Wilbur," said Wayne, "we have nothing to hide. All you have to do is ask us questions when you want to know something."

"Okay," I sneered, "what exactly are you doing to Sigma?"

"Are you implying that we're responsible for his transformation?" snapped Dr. Harrison. "Let me guess. You have evidence."

"As a matter of fact, I do. You two always stare at me when I enter the lab, and you're always whispering when I'm in the room. And you're good at science. You could have easily figured out how to turn a human into a lizard, and decided to keep me in the dark. You must want my company really badly!"

"Sir, that's ridiculous and you know it," said Wayne. "Why would we want to turn someone into a lizard? Our goal here is to cure cancer, not cause a transformation. Just because you're good at science doesn't mean you can 'figure out' how to turn someone into a lizard. That's not how biology works."

"With that logic, I might as well say that you're responsible for the transformation!" said Dr. Harrison pointing at the security guard. "You're always staring at people, aren't you?"

"Excuse me?" asked the security guard.

"How can I be certain you guys don't think I did it?" I asked.

"If you knew anything about science," said the scientist with the sling angrily, "I wouldn't be surprised. Or maybe there's something you're not telling us, huh?"

"No Bob," said Dr. Harrison. "Unless Wilbur has more PhDs than we do, he's careless, but not responsible for causing the transformation."

"Is that supposed to make me feel better!?" I snapped.

"Cut it out! All of you!" interrupted Janitor Tom. "It doesn't matter who's responsible. We need to focus on the task at hand…. We need to destroy that horrible creature."

"Seriously," I replied, pointing, "this guy is starting to creep me out."

Tom's right," said Wayne.

"He is?" I asked. "How?"

"But not about destroying Sigma," Wayne explained. "I think we're all partly responsible for what's happening to Sigma, so there's no point in blaming each other. Let's all focus on the task at hand, trying to find the cause of the transformation. That way we can figure out how to reverse it, or at least stop it," said Wayne calmly.

"You're doing my job for me, Wayne," said Jessica, sweetly smiling as she walked passed the security office.

"Wait a minute, Wayne," said Dr. Harrison, "you're forgetting that Wilbur snooped around in our offices!"

"Yeah, sorry for that."

"He didn't know we weren't hiding anything. I think it was

a perfectly logical response to all the stress he's been under," said Wayne, putting his hand on my shoulder. "It's okay, Sir."

"That's adorable," I said. "Now get your hand off me, and let's go to the lab."

Everyone took that as a sign to get to work. Janitor Tom glared at me before leaving the room. Jessica grabbed my shoulder as I started to head towards my office and said, "Wilbur, come with me."

I had no plans to undergo a counseling session again and told her so, probably in a ruder manner than I should have. I was on a mission—I had to go see Sigma.

"While you guys are in the lab doing whatever scientists do, I'm going to check on Sigma," I said, as everybody was leaving the lobby.

"I wouldn't go over there if I were you. They just woke him up," warned Wayne. "From what I've heard from my colleagues this morning, Sigma is furious. He found out that we removed his tumor. Plus, his head has started to change and he's in extreme pain."

"Well, now seems like as good a time as any to reassure him that we're working to help him." I walked ahead of the scientists before they could say anything else.

"His head is changing?" sighed Janitor Tom, as he walked past us. "Right on schedule."

I shot him a confused look, and kept going. What did he mean by 'Right on schedule?' When I got to the containment chamber, there were two security guards by the door.

"Sir," said one of them, "you're awfully brave coming down here. Sigma has been saying a lot of.. not so nice things about you."

"Just let me in," I quickly replied. There were only two guards and two scientists in the room. My eyes quickly fell on Sigma, who was lying on the ground in pain. Something looked strange about his head. I walked closer.

Saying Sigma looked worse was an understatement. The black spines on his head, arms, chest and back had grown longer. Some spines had sprouted from his chin too. His tail was now two feet long. His ears were purple and looked more like the webbed frills on a lizard. His nose was flat, and his face was slightly pulled out like a snout. It had a spiked bony plate on it like the skull I found in Janitor Tom's office. Sigma's cheeks were pulled back, revealing violet gums and sharp white fangs. On the back of his head were four growths which resembled horns. There was no doubt in my mind that Sigma's head was becoming the head of the creature.

How could this be happening? Was Tom right about history repeating itself? What exactly happened 50 years ago? I may never know. I gave up on explaining things the moment I met the Shadow Man. By the way, it's been weeks since I last saw him. I wonder where he is and what he's doing.

"Do any of you IMBECILES have a mirror?" asked Sigma. "I must see my FACE!"

One of the scientists opened a drawer and pulled out a hand mirror and slid it through the compartment under Sigma's door. Sigma slowly picked it up off the ground with a shaking clawed hand. He lifted it up towards his face and let out an ear piercing inhuman scream that could probably have been heard from the parking lot. He threw the mirror at the white tiled wall and it shattered into pieces.

"WHAT HAVE YOU DONE TO MY FACE!" growled Sigma. "THAT'S IT! YOU'RE GONNA PAY!!" His red eyes stared straight into mine. I knew Sigma wanted to leap at the glass, but he couldn't. He was in too much pain. The best he could do was bare his fangs and hiss.

"It's all your fault!" he snarled. "You're turning me into a lizard and you tore me open without asking. You're ruining my life! Once I get out of here, I'm going to ruin yours. You will suffer for what you've done!"

"Now, now Sigma. Calm down. No need to be so negative. We're friends here. We took out the tumor so we could figure out how to reverse your transformation."

"You're lying. And since when are we friends?" He spat. "I don't have any friends. Just enemies and you are one of them! As soon as I can stand again, I'm going to eat you!"

"Excuse me?" I asked.

"You heard me. I am going to eat you."

"Why would you want to do that?" Sigma simply growled in reply. A moment later he shrieked as another wave of pain hit him. I swear that I could actually see his head getting longer. When he turned, his tail looked like it was growing too. Sigma began to thrash around like a terrified fish.

"AH! HELP ME! HELP ME! MAKE IT STOP!" he snarled. "YOU'RE ENJOYING THIS, AREN'T YOU WILBUR?! MAKE IT STOP, SOMEBODY!"

"Can't you give him something?" I asked a scientist.

"We would Sir," he replied, "but the pain relievers we have are hardly working anymore. Not even morphine."

"WHAT!?" screamed Sigma.

"Just give him something," I demanded. "I don't want that poor animal to suffer? That's unthinkable! He's suffered enough! Give him the pain medication or you're fired!"

"But-" said the scientist.

"There are no buts at Helix! Only okay Sirs!"

"OH, SO I'M AN ANIMAL NOW?!" snarled Sigma.

The scientist looked at a security guard, who got out a tranquilizer gun. He opened the thick door and aimed at the thrashing Sigma. It took three darts before he fell asleep.

"You're both fired," was all I could say.

Eventually I got another scientist to give Sigma the pain medication he obviously desperately needed. I thought that would at least help him a little bit. I wish I could do more to ease his pain.

"How long will he sleep?" I asked.

"I don't know," said the scientist. "That dosage was intended for humans. I'd guess maybe a day." There was nothing more I could do here, so I finally went to my office. I had piles of paperwork and digital piles of emails, but I decided to just read a book. I'm the CEO, right? I can do what I want, can't I?

Towards the end of the day, Dr. Harrison came to my office to deliver an urgent report from the lab. "Am I intruding Sir?" he asked. I suddenly realized I had left my door open.

"No," I replied, sighing. "Come inside."

"Sir, I have the latest report from the lab. We've discovered the cause of the transformation."

"You don't sound very excited," I replied just as unenthusiastically. "What is it?"

"The white blood cells, Wilbur," he replied. "They're what's causing Sigma's metamorphosis."

"What do you mean?" I asked.

"As I said a while back, the creature's immune cells could travel anywhere in the body. That seemed natural. What isn't natural is that it seems like the cells were designed to transform anything they came in contact with into a creature like the one they came from. Remember how my team used the creature's genes to program Sigma's white blood cells to target cancer? They've... reached their target and then some."

"And then some?" I asked.

"Yes," Dr. Harrison continued, "the modified cells are spreading through Sigma's body rapidly, consuming not just the tumor, but all of his body cells. They're reproducing rapidly to form new ones. They appear to have turned into some kind of mobile stem cell. Stem cells that only eat what they don't recognize. I've never seen anything like this before! It's almost as if there are two organisms sharing his body, and one's overpowering the other."

"Fascinating," I said as the biology flew over my head. "Does this mean we can cure Sigma?"

"No," Dr. Harrison replied gravely. "I don't think there's anything we can do!"

I could tell that Dr. Harrison was trying as hard as he can to hold back his anger with me, but he did a good job trying to explain what had happened.

"Sigma's body systems have changed too," Dr. Harrison continued. "He's cold blooded. He now has two hearts, six lungs, three stomachs, and a few organs we can't even identify."

"I have a question that's been bugging me." I said. "Why is it now taking so many tranquilizer darts to knock him out?"

"His body chemistry has changed as well," said Dr. Harrison. "I just got a report from the containment chamber. Sigma's awake again and he's thrashing around. Neither the tranquilizer nor the pain medications worked. Such a poor soul."

"Speaking of souls, are Sigma's brain cells being consumed too?" I asked. "If they are then how come his consciousness still exists?"

"We believe they are, and have no explanation as to why his consciousness appears to have been preserved."

"Perhaps we've proved the existence of souls, Bill."

"Maybe," replied Dr. Harrison, who then moved on and said, "We also compared Sigma's DNA to the creature's DNA and discovered that the two were nearly identical."

"Could you sum this all up?" I asked

"In layman's terms," replied Dr. Harrison, "you may not have created the cells, but you're absolutely responsible for the transformation."

"Great," I sighed.

Dr. Harrison slapped down a stack of papers. "If you forget what I told you, read these," he groaned.

"One more question," I said.

"Make it quick."

"What did you mean when you said that the cells are not natural?"

"I mean that nature would never develop something like them. Their DNA must be written more like a computer program than a code for life. I think some unknown force created it."

"Weird," I replied, then asked, "Can you at least work on trying to cure Sigma?"

"As I said before," Dr. Harrison replied, "there's nothing we can do for that kid. He's too far gone."

"Do you want to be fired? If not, then try. Work weekends, nights, whatever it takes."

"Yes Sir," Dr. Harrison groaned as he left my office.

I sighed and picked up the phone to call human resources. I had a couple more disobedient employees in need of firing. Hopefully Dr. Harrison isn't next on the list.

Chapter 23

A Great Pet

<u>Thursday</u>

Human resources has been flooded with complaints from my employees lately. More so than usual. I don't think it's wrong of me to require them to work harder. Nothing gets done if you don't work hard. If they don't like how I run Helix Remedies, then why did they sign up in the first place? We're also are in a crisis, with the transformation going on downstairs and all. We have to work harder.

As I made my way to my office this morning, I came across a tour underway. I thought I canceled those long ago. It caught my interest. I recognized the man leading the tour. He was one of our scientists, and I'm guessing the woman and kids with him were his wife and children. Kids. Yuck. They started going down the stairs, so I followed them. As they got closer to the containment chamber, I ran in front of the family.

"Hello Sir," said the scientist. "How's it going?

"What are you doing?" I asked. "Tours were canceled weeks ago."

"I'm just showing my family around the place," he replied. "They haven't seen much of me lately, so I wanted to show them what I've been doing. You didn't used to have a problem with that."

"Well today it's different, George, with Sigma and all. I think you should wrap up your little tour and get out of here as soon as possible."

Suddenly, I noticed that his little boy had started to wander towards the containment chamber. He disappeared behind the door. I could hear a bunch of confused scientists yelling.

"Mommy, mommy!" said the kid. "Come quick! There's a lizard in here. A big one!"

I started running towards the containment chamber. When I got there, the scientists were trying to pry the kid off the glass. One of them was grabbing his shirt collar.

"Look at that lizard!" he squealed. "He'd make a GREAT PET!"

"A pet, huh?" snarled Sigma. "I'd make a wonderful pet. I'd guard the house. Even from the owners."

"He talks too," squealed the kid. "I want him!"

I looked at Sigma and saw that the transformation had progressed dramatically. Sigma's face had been fully pulled out into a snout, like a dinosaur, but with four nostrils. The bony plate on his snout was now spiked. I did a double take when I looked into his red eyes. He now had two pupils in each of them.

"Don't look at me!" Sigma snarled.

His horns had grown much longer and they were now also spiked. He had two large, long horns coming from his skull, and two small, short horns coming from behind his jaw. His purple ear frills had grown significantly longer and larger. They looked like dragon ears now. There were slits on his neck that opened and closed like a fish's gills would. Plus his hair now went down all the way down his back to his tail. Or were those feathers. And why were they purple?

"Would you kindly stop staring at me?!" Sigma asked again. His tail was almost as long as his body and his feet had changed too. They were longer and raptor-like, with sickle claws where his big toes should have been. The spines on his head, forearms, back, tail, and chest were also longer. Purple feathers had also sprouted from the spines on his arms. He had more muscle on him than he did as a human.

I somehow felt that I was staring at a fully transformed Sigma. This was the most surreal sight I have ever seen as a small town pharmaceutical CEO. When this hallucination is over, let me know.

"Can you creeps STOP staring at my new body already?!" Sigma hissed.

"George," I snapped, "I need you to leave NOW. And get your creepy kid out of here!"

"We gotta go, Timmy. We have a lizard just like this one at home, son,"

"But I want this one! He's big and he talks!"

"NOW, GEORGE!" I repeated. "Do you want to anger Sigma?!"

"Hey," said the kid. "Are you Dad's boss? You're a bad guy!"

"Kids never lie," said a security guard.

"You're both FIRED!" I roared. "And you kid, are PRE-FIRED from ever working here! So there!"

"You're right son, he is a bad guy," said George in shock. "Let's get out of here."

It was unsettling to watch George tell his wife what had just happened in only a few minutes. All five of them, including the security guard, left the room, chatting. I still have a lingering feeling from watching that. Is this what Counselor Jessica would call "guilt"?

"It seems I won't be the only one cheering when you're dead," Sigma hissed. "I can't help but agree with him. You're a very bad man. And I'm going to eat you for what you've done to me and what you've done to everyone else. I'm going to rid the world of you. It deserves a break from you."

I didn't say anything.

"A pet," whispered Sigma, scoffing at how ridiculous that thought was. I couldn't help but laugh at the thought too, but Sigma didn't see it that way.

"I am so going to kill you," he spat, "and it's not going to be quick either! This is no laughing matter! I went through more pain last night than any human has ever endured! You must suffer for what you've done to me!"

"Was that a death threat?" I asked. "You could be arrested for words like that."

"But I'm an animal now, aren't I? You can just dispose of me when you're through with your experiment. Forget the trial and the jail."

"That's not my plan. Why can't you just be nicer to me and trust me for once?"

"Every time I've seen a doctor, they've told me they'll cure my cancer. Every time, they've failed and given me a month less to live. I hate doctors, if you haven't realized that by now. I thought Helix would be different, but I was wrong. I've never met more cruel people on my life."

I kind of took offense to that, but didn't say anything. So Sigma wanted me dead. Well, he's not the first one to verbalize that. I seem to remember Subject Gamma being pretty angry too. Everyone at the lab remembers him because his teeth fell out, and then of course there was Delta. She was a crier who brought everyone down. Why can't we just have a normal person to deal with for a change? I'll be holding perhaps the strangest meeting in corporate history tomorrow: deciding what we're going to do about Sigma.

"Wilbur," called Sigma, "I want to eat you. I just can't decide if it should be for breakfast, lunch, or dinner. Maybe you can help me decide."

"How about none of the above," I called back as I headed to my office.

"What seasoning should I use on you? Salt? Pepper? It's going to take a lot of seasoning to get past your bitter taste."

I shook my head as I went through the door. Sigma could not be negotiated with anymore. When I returned to my office, there was another lab report on my desk. I just skimmed it, but got the information I needed. Apparently the mutant white blood cells the scientists found had finished their dirty work. Sigma's tumor was completely gone. The mutant cells had erased all evidence of themselves when they had completed Sigma's transformation. He might as well have always looked the way he does now. As Dr. Harrison solemnly stated in his report, "There's no humanity left in that poor soul."

After reading the report, I dealt with human resources and got those people fired officially. Apparently, you can't do paperwork for someone who doesn't work for you yet or is underage. At least I can still prevent that spoiled brat of a kid from ever working here. His name is in the database and listed as banned for life.

When the day had ended, I had two additional firings. One was a scientist who I overheard supporting Sigma's plan to eat me. The other was his secretary, who has a reputation for being totally loyal to him. I think they're dating or something. Perhaps they were just joking, but oh well. Good riddance.

As I was taking my evening stroll through the facility, I was tempted to stop at the containment chamber one more time. When I opened the door, I saw a couple of scientists right outside the window chatting. I was about to walk over to them to say hello when Sigma jumped at the glass, startling me. Both me and my heart jumped in response.

"Whoa," I said, "you startled me, Sigma."

"And you turned me into a lizard," hissed Sigma in response. "You deserve to be startled and then some. I'm going to eat you."

"Yeah," I yawned, "whatever."

All four pupils in Sigma's red eyes glared at me as I left the room.

Chapter 24

Nightmares

Well, Friday was quite a day. Where should I start? The day began with a long meeting to discuss what to do now that Sigma has been completely transformed. Nobody could seem to agree on what that would be.

We had one team that wanted to run experiments on him. Another group wanted to vivisect him because we sold our MRI a while back. Janitor Tom wanted us to burn him. Jessica's team wanted to study his psychology, and Marty suggested we turn him loose. I half wanted to turn him loose myself, but that didn't sound like a safe solution. I figured he might try to hurt people.

I ignored everyone's requests and decided that we'd keep him in the containment chamber untouched, indefinitely. I figured it was best not to tell Sigma my decision right away.

After I finished signing everyone's paychecks, and figuring out the budget, it was time for dinner. I pushed in my chair, grabbed my briefcase, and headed off the cafeteria. When I got there, I was in for a surprise. Counselor Jessica was behind the counter preparing food. I completely forgot that I had allowed her to be assigned to the cafeteria. During

128

her job interview, she talked about how much she liked to cook. In fact, cooking was her second job aboard the U.S.S. Enterprise. Because I had fired Chef, and Marty wasn't cut out for the job, I must have asked Laurie to assign anyone with experience to the kitchen. What was I thinking?

I was certain she was going to ask me about the counseling sessions I've skipped out on for two weeks in a row now. Sighing, I went to the back of the lunch line. When it was my turn, I took a deep breath.

"Hello Sir," greeted Jessica in a friendly voice.

"Hi...um...hi," I stuttered nervously.

"Would you like some chicken soup? It's my grandmother's recipe."

"Oh, sure, sounds good."

"I missed you again at today's counseling sess-"

"I apologize," I replied sarcastically. "I've been busy because of a particular transformation! I'll be sure to make it tomorrow!"

Jessica spooned some of the soup into the bowl on my tray. "You say that now Sir," said Jessica, reading me, "but I'm sure there will be another excuse tomorrow."

"You'll just have to wait and see," I replied with fake enthusiasm.

"Sir, these counseling sessions are for own good. You do realize that don't you?"

"Maybe, but they're not my thing."

"Perhaps. But you can't always expect your problems to solve themselves."

"Here, here," sighed Janitor Tom, who was right behind me in line.

"I'm holding up the line," I said. "See you later. Much later."

Jessica shook her head and got back to serving dinner. I slid my tray down the line, grabbed a few soup crackers, and a milk carton. I found a table in the corner and sat down. I listened to see if any of my employees were scheming against me, but I couldn't pick up anything. After a few minutes of listening, I took a few sips of the soup. Just as I was opening up the milk carton, I heard a voice from down the hallway.

"WILBUR! WILBUR!" screamed Marty, rounding the corner as fast as possible. His shoes squeaked on the concrete and he skidded over to my table, almost knocking over Dr. Wagner.

"Hey!" exclaimed Wayne. "Watch where you're going!"

"What is it Marty?" I demanded.

"He-e-e-e-e!" he whimpered.

"Alright, what's this new idea for a product that you just had to tell me about?"

"I-it's not a product!" Marty replied. "It's Sigma! H-e-He's-s escap-"

Before Marty could finish his sentence, a blaring alarm began to howl. Everybody jumped. A few people dropped their drinks. Glass shattered on the floor. Everyone in the room began to panic. Some people dove under the tables. Five security guards took off running in the direction Marty had come from. Everyone else started running towards the other exit, including Marty.

"What's going on?" asked a voice.

"I think Sigma got out!" said another.

"Is Brian alright down there?"

Suddenly I heard a couple gunshots from the hallway followed by a loud snarling.

"Goodbye Sir," cried Janitor Tom before running away.

"HE'S GOT ME!" yelled someone from the hallway.

"GET DOWN!" yelled a security guard, running into the room with a look of terror on his pale face. None of the other four guards were with him. I looked in the doorway and saw a gray humanoid reptile with hoop earrings on its purple frills, a shark tooth necklace, sharp claws, and red eyes. It was Sigma and he was holding a security guard with bleeding claw marks on his face and chest. The guard was struggling to get out of his grip.

When Sigma spotted me, he threw down the security guard, shoved the other one out of his way and came after me. Once I absorbed what was happening, I started running. I kicked aside a chair and table in my way and ran towards the door. It was like an obstacle course trying to get through the hallway outside. There were tables and chairs littering the ground. Somebody had also tipped over the watercooler. A scientist had already tripped over a folding chair.

"SIR!" he yelled. "Help! I think I broke my leg!"

I wanted to stop and help him up, but I had an angry lizard chasing me, so I kept going. I looked back and saw Sigma rush in and toss the furniture out of the way. He sunk his claws deep into the already injured scientist's back and threw him out of his way into the wall. The poor man yelped in pain.

I saw a whiteboard that nobody had knocked over yet and ran towards it. Sigma's red eyes stared straight into mine as I wheeled it into his way. I took off running, and turned when I heard a loud crash. Sigma had broken the whiteboard in half.

I hurried to the lobby, but a solid mass of humanity was struggling to pour out, leaving no room for the one person that Sigma was chasing after to escape. That's me. I couldn't even see the closet door where Janitor Tom and Marty were probably hiding again. As that thought crossed my mind, there were ear piercing screams. Sigma had caught up to me. I pushed through the crowd to make my escape.

Sigma knew what I was doing. The screams grew louder as Sigma viciously slashed and punched his way through the crowd, sending people scattering towards alternate exits.

Just as Sigma was about to grab me, I quickly plowed my way through the people. I turned the corner and ran to the staff offices. When I got to my office door, I opened it and locked it behind me. I immediately started stacking as many objects as I could against it. I pushed my desk over first. Then, all the file cabinets. Next I turned off the lights. Then I sat down on the floor and took a deep breath.

For what felt like half an hour, I heard dreadful screams coming from the halls. Obviously from people who were being tortured. I felt terrible knowing it was my fault. I never should have pursued the cure. I put my hands over my face and held my head low miserably.

What seemed like another half hour went by before the dreadful screams died down. I turned the light back on, and stared at the pile of objects blocking the door. There was no way I was moving those again. Not to mention I was worried that Sigma might still be just outside. I looked at the spot where my desk was and noticed a panel disguised with wallpaper. I remembered that it led to all off the staff offices on this side of the hallway, including Jessica's office. Behind her room was a fire door I could use to get out of the building.

I yanked the panel from the wall and crawled inside the tunnel. It was very dark with a musty odor. I hoped there weren't any mice back there. I took out my key chain and turned on the flashlight. The space was only three feet high. I had to avoid bumping my head on the cables, pipes, and vents above me as I crawled through. I counted five panels that went by until I reached the one that led to Jessica's office.

Pushing it open wasn't easy, because there was a bookshelf behind it. I shoved the panel as hard as I could. It came off and the bookshelf behind it crashed to the ground, scattering what were probably heavy psychology books everywhere. I found myself in Jessica's office. I sighed with relief when

I saw the red sign labeled "FIRE EXIT" that dimly lit the hallway outside. I got up and went to turn on the lights.

"Nice of you to join me," growled a voice that clearly wasn't Jessica's. "What seems to be the problem?"

I turned around and saw Sigma stretched out on the sofa. My heart started pounding. He had his elbows on an armrest and his clawed feet were resting on a stack of books. He smirked at me, showing his violet gums and pearly white fangs.

"Tell me about your nightmares, Wilbur," he sneered wickedly. "Maybe I can do something about them."

"HELP ME!" I finally screamed.

"They can't hear you, Wilbur. They're too busy being dead."

"You're not a very good liar."

Sigma got off the sofa and approached me. I took a few steps back.

"On the contrary," Sigma replied. "I learned from the best. You. And the best lie of all is that I'm only sixteen!"

"What?!" I asked, shocked. "That's illegal."

"That's right. I saw so much promise in your stupid cure that I actually broke the law to get in here. And you betrayed me! I put my life in your hands and for what? Just another disappointment. And this one is the worst of all. You turned me into a nightmare!"

"But I did cure your cancer!" I cried nervously.

"But you turned me into a NIGHTMARE!"

"It was an accident, I swear!"

Sigma started to lose it.

"Oh, so you accidentally turned me into a lizard. Got it. It's an accident that I have scales. An accident that I have talons instead of toenails. An accident that these… these demon horns grew out of my head? An accident that I have a tail? And you just accidentally cut the tumor out of my lung while I was AWAKE, accidentally leaving this giant scar on my chest! And that wasn't the only scar you have me. I have a whole lot more."

I looked up at Sigma's chest and sure enough there was a long violet-colored scar there. The scientists did surgery on him while he was awake? And didn't tell me? Did the tranquilizer really fail that badly? I felt pity for Sigma. That's sickening. Why would my staff do that?

"Oh my… Oh...I-I'm so sorry, Sigma," I replied with a stutter. "I'm deeply, genuinely sorry. I had no idea they did that. I didn't expect any of this to happen!"

"A LIKELY STORY!" Sigma growled. "APOLOGY NOT ACCEPTED! YOU WANTED ME TO SUFFER! THIS NEW BODY OF MINE WAS NO ACCIDENT! I DON'T LIKE IT! WHA- WHAT AM I? WHAT KIND OF SICK JOKE IS THIS!? I HATE YOU!"

"It's not my fault! You gotta believe-"

Sigma grabbed me by the throat and brought me closer to his face. "Drop your lies!" he growled. "What have you turned me into? Am I a weapon? An exotic pet? Tell me and perhaps I'll spare one of your limbs."

"What can I possibly say to convince you?" I whimpered. "All I wanted to do was cure your cancer.

"You didn't cure my lung cancer," snapped Sigma. "You gave me six lungs and these gills on my neck."

"I had no idea this would happen. Please, you have to believe me!"

"You're so stupid. Believe you?" hissed Sigma, laughing. "I don't have to do anything. I'm the one with the claws here. Not you. Me. Someone here's gonna die tonight, and it's certainly not going to be yours truly!"

Sigma slashed a claw across my cheek. I could feel pulses of pain and blood trickling.

"AH! WHAT WAS THAT FOR?" I cried.

"Believe me, you don't know pain like I do. Not yet. I'm

just getting started. When I am finished with you, you're going to be sorry you were even born."

"No need for that! Get your hands of me!" I yelled, trying to take back control.

"I'll let go of you when I feel like it. But first you will feel the same level of pain I have dealt with. Except unlike me, when it's over, you'll be dead. I'm gonna eat you."

"I've always wanted to lose some weight," I whimpered hysterically. That distracted Sigma just enough that his grip loosened. I struggled out of his grasp and ran out into the hallway towards the warehouse. I was under too much stress to remember the fire exit was right next to me.

"WE'RE NOT DONE, WILBUR!" Sigma spat, as I sped away. "WE'RE NOT DONE!"

He had taken off running as well. I could hear his talons clicking on the linoleum floor. As I aimlessly ran through the hallways, I avoided my moaning employees, who were littering the floor. Thank goodness they were still alive.

The only exit in my direction was in the warehouse. I slid through the doorway leading to it, then looked behind me to check if Sigma was still following me. I had run a surprisingly long way. Strangely, Sigma was not behind me.

There were racks filled with pallets, barrels, and crates as far as the eye could see, but no Sigma. I started to panic. Where could he be? I scanned the room for a hiding place or an exit, but the train platform was what caught my eye. Suddenly, the intercom turned on. Oh, thank goodness. Somebody's still alive in here. My sense of relief faded away when I heard the voice over the intercom.

"I'm gonna to eat you, Wilbur," echoed Sigma. "You're not even worth the ground you walk on! You're nothing but trouble! In fact, your only purpose in life is to cause problems and then be eaten! Like a rat, a roach, or some other bug."

"And that's what you think of the guy who cured your cancer?!" I yelled.

"You didn't cure my cancer. You turned me into a monster. I can never go back to life the way it used to be. And for that you will pay!"

"Pay? I don't think I can fit that in the next budget," I cried hysterically.

"With your life, you idiot," replied Sigma's venomous voice. The intercom turned off.

"Sigma?" I asked.

There was no answer. I slipped outside onto the train platform. My intention was to get to the recycling center on the other side of the rail yard where I'd be able to call the cops. There is an emergency phone over there, and it's right by the tracks. I just had to get over there.

It was pitch black outside except for the lights hanging on the brick wall and in the rail yard. All I could hear was the chirping of crickets and the pounding of my heart. Just when I felt a sense of relief, a voice sneered, "Pleased to eat you!"

I turned around just as Sigma pounced on me, slamming me to the ground. I tried to push him off, but he was too strong. "I'm giving you one more chance to admit your guilt!"

"N-no!" I panicked. "I did nothing wrong! I-it was an accident, I swear!"

Sigma snapped both of my arms, leaving me pounding with pain.

"That's for luring me into this sick place!" he snarled. I wanted to struggle out of his grip, but for some reason, I feared my arms would fall off, so I didn't move. Sigma turned me on my side and I cried out in pain. Then he shredded my back with his claws.

"That's for all the injections!"

I could feel the blood flowing from my wounds, and started to become light headed.

"Oh, are you crying?" Sigma asked. "Good. Keep those tears flowing!"

Sigma then punched me in the face, breaking my nose. He shredded my chest next. I was screaming in pain at this point.

"You're in terrible pain, aren't you. This could all end now. I'll spare your life if you order your scientists to turn me back into a human. Think about it."

I had a decision to make. I realized that if I told the truth I would die, but if I lied and said there was a chance, I could possibly save myself. But my scientists had been through so much. They had lost so much time with their families. I couldn't do that to them again. I couldn't push them further, even if there was a chance that Sigma could be turned back.

At that moment, I decided enough was enough. I wasn't going to selfishly accept another offer from the Devil. Not for $5 million. Not for my life. It was time to end it. "Kyle," I said. "I do not accept."

"WHAT!?" the creature snarled angrily. "Are you trying to be heroic or something?! That's adorable! And who are you calling KYLE?! WHO IS KYLE?! My name is SIGMA! Always has been!"

"Okay Sigma. The scientists said there's nothing we can do for you, and I believe them. Do what you have to do to me."

"Very well then. Prepare to die."

Sigma bit down into my shoulder and started to gnaw on me viciously, like he was a mountain lion or something. My pain was starting to numb. Was he really eating me, like he said he would? Oh well, I thought. I'll never know. I was ready to die.

"AND THAT'S FOR EVERYTHING!"

As my consciousness began to fade, I heard a train horn in the distance.

"Chew, chew!" Sigma laughed madly as he bit down on my arm.

Sigma smiled wildly, and suddenly dragged me over to the edge of the platform. He held me above the shiny rails. He hesitated for a second. The last thing I remember is hearing a deafening train horn, the rumbling of a locomotive and seeing a freight train fly past the loading dock. I also heard several clicking sounds.

"Drop him!" commanded a stern voice.

I fell to the ground and the lights went out.

Chapter 25

Five Million Apologies

<u>Sunday</u>

I awoke to find myself sitting in my office. Strange. I looked around and everything was in perfect detail. Nothing was stacked by the door. Everything was where it should have been. Suddenly, I spotted a familiar figure in the shadows. The Shadow Man.

"You!" I snapped. I got out of my seat and grabbed him by his shoulders.

"Can you explain just what the heck is going on? Where are we?"

"We're nowhere Wilbur," he replied cryptically. "Now please let go of me."

"Why'd you bring me here?"

"On the contrary, you brought us here, Wilbur."

"Am I dead?" I asked. "Aren't you going to give me an out of body experience? Let me see myself on the operating table?"

"So many questions," replied the Shadow Man.

"I asked you a question! Am I dead?"

"I wouldn't be lying if I said you were very much alive."

"Then if I'm alive, why can't you wake me up?"

139

"We felt that now would be the best time to tell you that you have succeeded," said the Shadow Man. "You have cured cancer and you'll be receiving $5 million."

"I didn't cure cancer!" I yelled. "I turned a teenager into a lizard!"

"We never mentioned that was not allowed."

"You! You're the one who caused all my problems!"

"No. You caused all your problems," explained the Shadow Man. "You could have declined my offer at any time. We weren't actually hoping for a cure for cancer. We wanted to see how you would react under stress with the promise of material wealth, and you put on a good performance."

"So, I am just a test subject in your little experiment?" I asked.

"In a manner of speaking. We're very much alike, you and I. You use test subjects as well."

"Can you turn Sigma back?"

"With great difficulty we could, but we will not. You have provided us with our next test subject."

"Okay, so you guys are scientists. I get that," I said, "but from where?"

"I'm going to leave that one for you to figure out," replied the Shadow Man. "Maybe the man with the broom could help you."

"We really must leave," warned a woman's voice from the hallway. "You're telling him too much, and his people may figure out we're here."

"So long, Wilbur," said the Shadow Man. "You have been a fascinating test subject."

"Now wait just a minute!" I yelled. "I'm not letting you go until you promise to never bother me again!"

"I'm afraid we can't do that," responded the Shadow Man. "The experiment is never over."

My office blurred out and everything around me turned

white. I started to make out several tall figures standing around me.

"Am I dead?" I asked. "It's about time already!"

I looked around and faces started coming into focus. I saw Dr. Wagner, Dr. Harrison, and Marty hovering over me. There were many other doctors and scientists in there as well. A few guards and cops were there too. Everybody in the room cheered. I thought I was hallucinating. People cheering?... At Helix?... For me?

"No, Wilbur," said Dr. Wagner. "You're very much alive. But you scared us a couple times."

"I thought we were going to be haunted by your ghost!" added Dr. Harrison, smiling for the first time in a while. "That would've been terrifying."

I tried to move, but I couldn't. "AH!" I yelled. "I'M PARALYZED!"

"No you're not. Your arms and legs are flailing. Now hold still before you break any more bones."

"Failing?"

"No, flailing." I suddenly realized I was in a body brace and stopped trying to get out.

"How long have I been unconscious?" I asked.

"Just a day," Wayne replied.

"Do you know where Sigma is?"

"No, we don't know where he is," said the Sheriff, who was also in the room. "He hopped onto a passing freight train after we stormed the building."

"So you're saying he could be anywhere?!" I yelled trying to sit up in the bed. "How do you know he won't try to MURDER me again?!"

"Easy, Wilbur," said Wayne, setting me back down. "You broke a lot of bones out there."

As I settled back down into the bed all kinds of things started going through my mind. What if Sigma finds me again? How are the other people he hurt? Are there going to be lawsuits because of this? "What are the casualties out of this incident?" I asked.

Wayne told me that in addition to myself, Sigma had attacked at least half of the staff. There were eighteen people hospitalized with serious injuries, one with a broken back; but thankfully nobody was killed.

"S-Sir," said Wayne nervously. "There's... something I have to tell you. The day we removed the tumor, we thought that one dart would keep Sigma knocked out but we were wrong. When we started the surgery Sigma bolted awake. We had to put him back under, but he was left with a scar."

"I know," I replied. "Sigma told me about it. I saw the scar."

"I decided to leave that out of the report. I was afraid you wouldn't believe me. Please believe me now Sir! It was an accident!"

"I believe you, Wayne. I spent a lot of time with someone who was convinced I was lying and couldn't see otherwise. I wouldn't wish that on you."

Dr. Harrison unexpectedly came over, holding a bank statement. "Sir," said Dr. Harrison, "we were hoping you could shed some light on this. Somebody deposited $5 million into the company account. We have no idea who it was. We called the bank, and they said it wasn't a mistake."

"Do you have a rich uncle or something?" I asked.

"No, I don't," he replied. "Do you?"

"No I don't have an uncle."

"Well, did the money come from your father?" asked Dr. Harrison.

"No, he is retired now and doesn't have that kind of money."

"Looks like that Shadow Man of yours is real. So you had a valid reason to make me work weekends, didn't you? Sorry I doubted you Sir, but you're still the most reckless person I know."

I was puzzled at Dr. Harrison's new sense of humor, as dry as it was. He had always been a very humorless person. Oh well, nice change of pace.

"I'll admit I thought he was a construct of your mind too," said Wayne. "We all thought you imagined him under stress. I'm sorry. We all are."

"Guys," I sighed, "I want y'all to know that I made some mistakes. My biggest one was not having faith in all of you. I didn't realize it at the time, but during the cancer cure project, you proved me wrong. You guys and gals worked harder than ever. The fact that you saved my life proves you are good people too.

"I never should have accepted the Shadow Man's offer. We would have figured out a way to save the company. Instead, I indirectly inflicted horrible injuries on numerous people, gave false hope to our test subjects, robbed you of your personal lives, and ruined the life of a young man. I'm sorry. If you want me to leave, I'll pack up my things and get out of here. I deserve it. I'm nothing but trouble."

There was an awkward silence like never before. Everybody stared. "No," said Dr. Wagner, breaking the silence. "Don't leave. We're a family here at Helix. Families take care of each other."

"The place wouldn't be the same without your interesting way of running things," added Dr. Harrison.

I couldn't help but laugh. "So," I chuckled, "I guess there never was a mutiny after all."

"Oh there was," replied Dr. Harrison, smiling. "It's just off for the time being."

"I hope it stays that way. So where do we go from here?" I asked.

"Well first we should decide whether or not to continue the cancer cure project."

"We're done. I want the creature's body and the cure

incinerated. Tom was right and I should have listened to him. Nobody should ever have to go through what Sigma went through. As for the money, I want half of it to go into a special account for anyone harmed by Helix Remedies. The rest will go to the company."

"I like this guy," said Janitor Tom. "Much nicer than the old Wilbur."

"What's with the sudden change of heart?" asked Dr. Harrison.

"You try being nearly eaten by your worst fear and see how that changes you."

"I guess our counseling sessions are over. I think you're cured," said Jessica.

"Thank goodness," I replied. "Now I can spend more time actually doing productive things, like planning our ice cream social!"

Everybody sighed with relief. Just the looks on their faces showed that they cared about me. I guess you don't need money to fix your company. Instead, you need a good guy running it.

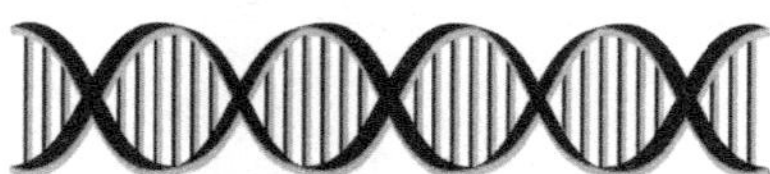

Sigma's Bookshelf (www.SigmasBookshelf.com) is an independent book publishing company that exclusively publishes the work of teenage authors, who are between the ages of 12 - 19. The company was founded in 2016 by Minnesota teenager Justin M. Anderson, whose first book, *Saving Stripes: A Kitty's Story*, was published when he was 14, and has since sold hundreds of copies.

"I know there are a lot of other teenagers out there who are good writers and deserve to have their work published, but don't have access to the kinds of resources I do. I wanted to help them," he said.

Sigma's Bookshelf is a sponsored project of Springboard for the Arts, a nonprofit arts service organization. Contributions on behalf of Sigma's Bookshelf may be made payable to Springboard for the Arts and are tax deductible to the extent permitted by law. Donations can be made online at www.SigmasBookshelf.com/donate.